THE LAST STOP

A Dear Abby Cozy Mystery - Book 4

SONIA PARIN

ISBN-13: 978-1720177074

❄ Created with Vellum

Chapter One

"And this is where I picked up Doyle." Abby slowed down and pointed at the side of the road. "I think he'd been trying to get across the road but collapsed from exhaustion. He had a layer of mud on him and could barely whimper." Abby continued on her way, making sure she didn't exceed the speed limit. "Isn't the scenery pretty, Mom? Winding roads. Lush green trees." Abby hummed under her breath.

She'd spent the last twenty-four hours in the air, and on the road, making her way from Iowa, to LAX, and finally, to Melbourne airport. She'd now been driving for three hours on this last stretch of road leading to the small alpine town of Eden. Soon, she'd arrive in her adopted home.

"The trees are whizzing by again, Abby. I think you're driving too fast."

Swirling the cell phone to face her, Abby saw her mom frown and shake her head.

Abby smiled. "You wouldn't say that if you were sitting in the car with me. The cell phone distorts images."

"Please keep both hands on the steering wheel and set the phone straight again. I need to see where we're going."

Abby readjusted the cell to face forward just as her mom yelped.

"Watch out for kangaroos."

Abby laughed. "Nothing to worry about, Mom. Those signs are everywhere. I've yet to spot a kangaroo. Apparently, they come out at night. We'll be right."

"Still, you should slow down."

If they did, they'd never get there. Belatedly, Abby wished she hadn't propped the cell phone on the dashboard where her mom could get a full view of the road ahead.

"You've had a long flight," her mom continued. "I think you should have taken a day off to catch up on your sleep. Three hours is a long time to drive."

"I slept on the plane, Mom. And, I made a couple of pit stops."

"You put your cell phone on airplane mode. I don't know what you did during all those hours."

"I didn't have a choice, Mom." Seeing the *Welcome to Eden* sign, Abby straightened. Home at last, she thought. Her two-week mini vacation to visit her mom in Iowa had been exhausting. Everyone in town had wanted to catch up with her and hear about her tales from down under. Abby had done her best to paint a rosy picture but her mom had interjected at every opportunity, reminding everyone about Abby's first day in Eden.

"Fancy flying half way around the world and stumbling upon a dead body," Abby mouthed under her breath. "I fear for my daughter's life. That town is plagued with killers."

"What was that?" her mom asked.

"Nothing, Mom."

"Promise you won't disconnect me."

Abby couldn't help cringing. Her mom had dropped off several times but now that they were getting close to the township the connection had become stable. "We'll be fine once I can switch over to wi-fi. I'll need to recharge my cell phone. Faith will have the laptop all set up. I made sure of that. Besides, why would I disconnect you? That would defeat the purpose."

Somehow, she had to make her mom believe the small town of Eden was as safe as anywhere else. In fact, safer. Everyone had been put on notice. Behave, or else... "You'll see for yourself soon enough. Eden is an idyllic little town where everyone knows my name."

"How could they not know your name. When you first arrived, everyone thought you were a killer."

Abby grinned. "They only suspected me for a couple of hours." Reaching for the cell phone, Abby held it up.

"We're about to arrive. I don't want you to miss this." She slowed down and pointed out the pub where she lived. "That's the Gloriana."

"It would be impossible to miss it," her mom said. "Has it always been painted red? Oh, and look, you weren't kidding about the ship's figurehead hanging by the door."

"Yes, as I told you, it came from a shipwreck. The first Faydon to travel out to Australia in the 1800s nearly lost his life when his ship was caught in a storm. He organized a rescue team to haul the figurehead out and then he carted it all the way inland to Eden. Although, at the time, the town was nothing but an idea waiting to be seeded." Slowing down, she parked her car and breathed a sigh of relief. She'd made it in one piece. "We'll go in first. I need to recharge my phone. Then I need to get Doyle." She'd arranged for Doyle to have sleepovers at the vet's but her office assistant, Faith, had taken him during the day.

They'd arrived just after the lunchtime rush hour so Abby didn't expect to find many people at the pub. Leaving her luggage in the car, she strode in and nearly jumped out of her skin.

A chorus of welcome home exclamations greeted her. Half the town had shown up at the pub and crowded around her.

"Oh, my. This is overwhelming," her mom said. "Look at all these people."

Abby made her way to the counter. Before she

reached it, Faith rushed toward her and threw her arms around her. While Abby had been on vacation, her office assistant had been holding the fort at the Eden Rise Gazette where they both worked. They'd chatted almost every day and Abby had been surprised to feel pangs of home sickness for the town she had landed in only a few months before.

"You're back. You have no idea how much we missed you. Everything has been so dull since you left."

Really?

"What's going on?" her mom asked. "I can't see anything."

"Faith. You're still hugging me and I can barely breathe."

"I know. I've just missed you so much."

"Okay. I'm back and I'm not alone." When Faith stepped away, Abby held up her cell phone. "My mom's here."

Everyone waved and called out a hello.

"Hang on, if you're here, where's Doyle?" Abby looked around her.

Faith pointed toward the fireplace. Being on the other side of the world meant she'd left summer behind and had stepped straight into the middle of winter.

Doyle had clambered up onto Markus Faydon's shoulder. The pub's co-owner emerged from his special chair by the fireplace, his perpetual scowl in place as he re-united Abby with Doyle.

Wrapping him in her arms, Abby lapped up Doyle's

excitement to see her again. "Here's my boy." As she lavished him with attention, she caught sight of the local health inspector. He'd been the first local to turn a blind eye and bestow Doyle with special privileges at the pub to come and go as he pleased, so long as he stayed away from the kitchen. Abby smiled and thought the warm reception would go a long way toward setting her mom's mind at ease.

"Did you bring my laptop?" Abby asked.

Nodding, Faith waved her toward the counter. "It's all set up."

"Good." Holding up her cell phone, she smiled at her mom. "I'll have to disconnect you for a bit, Mom. But I'll get you back online on the laptop. Talk to you soon." She disconnected the video chat and sank down on a stool. "You have no idea what it's been like having my mom with me during the drive over. At least on the plane I had the excuse of putting the cell on airplane mode. I've never seen my mom so jittery. Would you believe she got car sick?"

Mitch Faydon, the co-owner of the pub Abby lived in, smiled. "Beer?"

"Yes, please." She checked her watch. "I think I'm going to sleep for twenty-four hours. This should help." Abby looked around her. "I can't believe all these people turned up to welcome me back."

Mitch cleared his throat. "Actually, they didn't."

"Huh? Did you rent a crowd?

"Most of them are tourists. Their bus broke down so I'm putting them up until it's fixed."

"Oh, I see." Abby plugged her phone to the computer so it could recharge.

"What was that? I only heard half of it," her mom said as Faith connected the video chat on the laptop.

When Abby explained about the tourists, her mom's interest perked up. "That would be fun. Can we go on a bus tour?"

Abby had already scheduled a few sightseeing trips around the area but since she'd made it her priority to keep her mom happy, she agreed.

"I'll look into it and take care of all the details," Faith said.

Her mom yelped. "What's he doing here? Has someone been murdered?"

Turning, Abby saw Detective Joshua Ryan making a beeline for her. "Mom, he's just here to say hello." She hoped.

"Hello, Eleanor. How was your trip over?" Joshua asked.

"Puzzling. I still don't understand why y'all have to drive on the wrong side of the road. Knowing about it is one thing. Seeing it for myself... Well, it's disconcerting."

Joshua straightened his tie and winked at Abby. "Eleanor, you're down under now. Everything is on the other side. Your right is our left and your up is our down. All those states you have up north, we have them

7

down south and all the sunny states you have down south, we have them up north. Even the water swirls down the drain in the opposite direction. I know it all sounds topsy-turvy, but you'll get used to it in no time."

When his cell phone rang, he excused himself.

"Is that a crime in progress call?" her mom asked. "Abby? What's going on? Did someone get killed?"

"No, Mom." The town had been put under strict orders to be on its best behavior. Faith had promised she would spread the word around...

"You have nothing to worry about, Eleanor. Statistically speaking," Mitch said, "Our town is the safest place to be in. In fact, up until your daughter showed up, we had a clean record with zero crimes."

"Are you suggesting trouble follows my daughter around?" her mom asked.

Mitch shifted. "Well, some people believe what you think about, you bring about. When Abby first arrived, she wanted to establish herself and make an impression on her new employer. Her thoughts would have been focused on getting a scoop and she did." Mitch grinned.

Her mom's eyes widened. "Yes, by discovering a dead body."

Abby rolled her eyes. "Not helping, Mitch," she mouthed. Seeing the detective step back inside the pub, she strode over to him. "Joshua. Please tell me there isn't a crime in progress. I told you, I need two weeks. If anything happens while my mom is visiting, you need to sweep it under the rug." Abby looked over her shoulder at the laptop on the counter. "My mom will be keeping a close eye on absolutely everything."

"You actually said that with a straight face," Joshua smiled. "Your mom's not exactly here."

"This is a practice run. It will only work if we all do our bit and pretend that she is here."

Taking her elbow, Joshua drew her aside.

"What?"

"Don't look now. You're being filmed."

Slanting her gaze toward the bar, Abby looked at the mirror and caught the reflection of a couple of people holding up their phones and aiming them toward her.

"They're with that tourist bus that broke down," Joshua explained.

"Why are they filming me?"

Joshua lowered his head and smiled. "Well... They've been in town for a couple of days and Mitch has been entertaining them with stories about you."

Her voice hitched. "Why would he do that?"

"Because they asked. Joyce got the ball rolling when they stopped by the café while the local mechanic towed the bus away. You can't blame them for trying to cash in on the opportunity. Most tourist buses drive straight through Eden on their way up to Bright and the ski slopes. That's a lot of tourist dollars driving by. Relax. They should be on their way soon. Come on, let's go get you a beer. I'm buying."

Abby's eyebrows drew downward. "I'm being used as a tourist attraction."

~

Abby peeled an eye open and stared straight into Doyle's large brown eyes. "I guess I made it upstairs." She looked around to make sure she'd landed in the right room. "Please tell me that's the sun shining in my face and I slept right through the night." She gave Doyle a scratch behind the ear. "Yeah, I know. If you could talk, you'd tell me. Okay. I'm awake now and I'm going to assume it is morning and you want to be fed because the alternative is that it's several mornings later and you were just about to take a bite out of me."

She reached for her cell phone. The whole idea of her mom joining her on a virtual visit was to actually have her around throughout the entire day so she might as well get used to it.

"Hey, how did I get to my room? I only had a couple of beers and I remember asking you to lead the way. Did you herd me back?" Abby sat up. "Hang on. I think I might have tried to go into another room by mistake. I remember apologizing." She groaned. She supposed the jet lag had already caught up with her...

"Okay. This is weird. I can't get a connection." After several more attempts and failing, she decided to feed Doyle, have a shower and get some food into her and then try to connect the video chat.

Half an hour later, she made her way downstairs and headed toward the dining room. Along the way, she bumped into Mitch. "Hey. Is something wrong with the internet this morning? I'm trying to get my mom on-line."

"It's working perfectly fine," Mitch said.

"There must be something wrong." Abby gasped. Had something happened to her mom? "She's not answering. She always answers."

"Who?" Mitch asked.

"My mom."

"Oh. She came down earlier."

"Huh?"

Mitch grinned. "I'm trying to get into the spirit of it all. Your virtual mom came down about an hour ago."

"What are you talking about?" Abby waved her cell phone. "She can't have come down by herself."

"You must be jet lagged. She's in the dining room."

Abby swayed.

"Are you right there?"

"Please explain."

"Last night, she exchanged numbers with a few people from the tour group and arranged to connect with them this morning." Mitch clicked his fingers in front of her eyes. "*Wakey-wakey.* Remember, when your cell phone recharged, you handed it over to the person sitting next to you and your mom made the rounds so she could chat with people."

Swinging around, Abby rushed toward the dining room and called out, "Who has my mom?"

Several people turned to look at her.

"Mom?" Abby called out again.

"Over here, Abby."

"That's her," someone said.

Seeing a group of diners all huddled together, Abby approached their table. "Excuse me, please. I believe you have my mom."

"They've been keeping me company while you slept, Abby." Her mom introduced the group. The names went in one ear and out the other but Abby noticed they all wore name tags, to make the tour bus driver's life easier, one woman explained.

"You go on and have your breakfast. I'll be fine here," her mom assured her. "They've been telling me about all the places they've visited. Would you believe it? They'll be traveling right around the country. Go on. We'll catch up later."

Abby stepped back. Feeling slightly dazed, she strode over to a table.

"Looks like your mom ditched you," Markus said in his gruff tone. "Makes you wonder what they have that you don't."

"I hate to admit it, but I do feel slighted." Abby glanced over at the group. "Could I have breakfast and lots of it, please." Doyle curled up by her feet and settled into one of his morning snoozes. Noticing Markus still hovering by her table, she looked up. "I'm giving you carte blanche. You can bring me whatever you want."

Markus rested his hand on her shoulder. "I'm sure

you're still her little girl. You know, sometimes, parents need to enjoy their own space."

"Markus. The carte blanche gave you freedom to bring me whatever you like for breakfast."

He grinned. "Think of the advice as an added extra. Here at The Gloriana we make customer satisfaction our number one priority. Right along with ensuring it remains a crime free zone. Yes, we're big on that too. Did I say that right?"

Rolling her eyes, she shooed him away.

As she waited for her breakfast, Abby tried to distract herself by reorganizing the sugar satchels but her gaze kept skipping over to the next table. She could hear her mom laughing and joking with someone named Alice and exchanging a recipe with Steph. Linda had spent some time in Iowa City where her husband had been a visiting professor. There were a couple of other women but Abby didn't notice them saying much.

Abby sighed. Sometimes, she forgot her mom had a life of her own. Abby's dad had passed on when she'd been a toddler so it had always been just the two of them. When Abby had moved to Seattle for work, she'd worried her mom would miss her but she hadn't. After all, she had her job. Being a children's book illustrator kept her busy throughout the year and she had her friends and neighbors. Since moving half way around the world, however, her mom had grown overly protective and worried about Abby's wellbeing.

"Breakfast of champions," Markus said as he set a plate down in front of her.

"*Huevos Rancheros*?" Abby asked.

"Close enough. Eggy Vegetarian Delight with Savory Oatmeal."

"I see." Abby tried to sound impressed but failed miserably.

Markus smiled. "The way I see it, Hannah has taken oatmeal to a whole new level. Instead of sugar and cinnamon, she seasoned the oatmeal with salt and pepper and topped it with a variety of lightly sautéed chopped vegetables and a sunny side up egg. Enjoy." Markus set down a piece of paper on the table. "When you finish, we'd appreciate your feedback."

Looking up, she saw Markus trying to smile but his perpetual scowl won out.

Abby looked down at the form. "Customer feedback? I'm guessing Mitch came up with this idea."

"I always knew the day would come and I'd have to own up," Markus sighed. "Yes, I did drop him on his head. Call me clumsy."

"Wow. I go away for two weeks and come back to this." While Markus strode off growling under his breath, Mitch stopped by her table, a huge grin on his face.

"How's the morning after treating you?" he asked.

"I'm guessing I drunk one too many beers but it worked a treat. I slept right through the night." She held up the customer feedback form. "What's this?"

"Oh, yes. Remember to fill that out, please. Markus and his bright ideas. I'm trying to humor him. You know he can be as grumpy as a bear with a sore head."

The edge of her lip kicked up. "I thought it might have been your sister's idea."

"Eddie? Oh, no. She's focusing on her own stuff. Now she's in competition with us. Her restaurant is stealing all our best customers. Who would have thought with a name like Posh and Bull? Anyhow, we'd appreciate your honest opinion." He looked down at her plate and grimaced. "That's what Markus tried to impress you with? I told him to play it safe and stick with bacon."

Hearing her mom calling her, Abby turned and saw one of the tourists waving his phone at her. "Your mom wants to connect with you now."

Abby propped her cell phone against a sugar bowl. "I guess I won't be eating breakfast alone after all." Her mom proceeded to tell her all about the new people she'd met and appeared to have taken a liking to Mr. Howington.

"Bert's a retired accountant." Her mom lowered her voice. "You won't believe this. He won a lottery jack-pot. That's how he funded his trip for himself and his friends. They're actually avoiding the large cities and weaving their way from one small town to the next. Alice, that's one of the women in the group, is a history buff so she has all these tidbits to share. They'll be trav-eling around for several months."

"And Mr. Howington is picking up the tab? Wow. That's generous."

Her mom gave a pensive nod. "So, what's on the agenda for today?"

"I thought we might start with a proper tour of the town. We'll drop in on all the stores and I can introduce you to the locals. Let me know when you feel like calling it a day. The time difference takes some getting used to."

"Oh, I'll be fine. I've changed all the clocks to Australian time."

Abby finished her breakfast and washed it all down with coffee.

"Remember to fill out the customer feedback form," her mom said as she appeared to be looking over Lexie's shoulder.

Turning, Lexie saw the tourists' group organizing themselves to leave.

"They must have found another bus to take them on a day trip."

Noticing a hint of interest in her mom's voice, Abby said, "I get the feeling you'd like to go with them."

"Nonsense. I'm here to spend time with you."

"That's lovely, Mom, but… if you want to go, I do have some work I need to catch up on."

"Really? You won't mind?" She didn't wait for Abby to answer. "Call Bert over."

"Bert?"

"Mr. Howington."

Bert Howington jumped at the chance to take Abby's mom along on a virtual tour saying, "I'm going to have a tale and a half to tell when I get home."

One of the women held out her cell phone and asked Abby to take a photo of them.

"Abby, take a photo for me too," her mom called out.

Promising to be back by dinnertime, the tour group left on their day trip taking her mom along with them.

"You look worried," Mitch said.

"I feel worried. What if something happens?" Abby had planned this virtual tour right down to the last detail, leaving nothing to chance. She wanted to make a positive impression on her mom so she'd come down and visit her for real. Surging to her feet, she said, "I think I might follow them at a discreet distance. Come on, Doyle. We don't want to lose sight of them."

Chapter Two

"*I* lost them," Abby wailed. She'd been doing so well, following the tourist bus at a discreet distance. It had been easy enough to do along the long stretches of country road, but then the bus had made a turn heading further up the mountain and along a winding road.

Sighing, Abby slowed down and checked her cell phone for directions. She'd definitely missed a turnoff. Either that or they'd taken a different route to the next town. "Okay, we might as well head back. I wouldn't mind a second breakfast."

Doyle huffed out a breath and sank his head between his paws.

"Hey, I'm not blaming you. Did you hear me say anything? It's not your fault if nature calls. I had to stop for you." She gave him a scratch under his chin and turned back toward town. "It's just as well. I really should catch up with what's been going on. And you know what that means... Yes, I'm going to Joyce's Café. Well, maybe not straight away."

As she drove back, Abby rehearsed what she would have said if her mom had been with her. "Let's see... This is the dirt road Doyle and I turned into when we were looking for Kinsley Roberts. She has a magnificent house. Although, if you'd seen it then, you would not have agreed. Yes, we did find a dead body." Abby shrugged. "It's not as if we went looking for trouble." Tilting her head, she tried to remember if she'd told her mom about Joyce blacklisting her and refusing to sell her coffee until she discovered the identity of the *Eden Bloggess*. "My memory is a bit hazy." Yes, she'd gone through withdrawal symptoms, surviving on limited coffee rations for several days. At first, she had considered using the opportunity to wean herself and switch from coffee to tea. While she'd tried to make the best of the situation, she hadn't quite embraced the idea of becoming a tea drinker.

"What do you think, Doyle? Should I make a permanent switch over to tea? It would be a bold move. I'm sure Joyce would issue a swift reprisal and accuse me of inciting rebellion within the community because, of course, I wouldn't simply stop drinking coffee. I would make sure everyone knew about it with an article on the front page of the Eden Rise Gazette expounding the benefits of tea drinking. She has it coming. The woman had me on tenterhooks when she blacklisted me. Faith is right. She has way too much power, which she wields with the wrath of a Goddess." Laughing under her breath, Abby heard a text message coming through. "Oh, it's Mom." Abby pulled over and answered the text. Moments later, she received a response.

"Okay. Looks like she wants a break from the tour group." Checking the roaming signal, she connected the video chat and slipped the cell phone into the cradle she had customized for her dashboard. "Mom."

"Oh, I see you're out and about."

"Yes." She didn't want to admit she'd tried to follow the tourist bus, so she prevaricated. Actually, she lied. "I wanted to check out the progress at Kinsley's house. Work is well under way."

"Is that the house where you found a dead body?" her mom asked.

Abby bobbed her head from side to side. Yes, she had found a dead body, but not on purpose. Abby shifted in her seat and decided to change the subject. "How are you feeling?"

"Jetlagged."

Her armchair traveling mom... Jet lagged? "Did you enjoy hanging out with the tourist group?"

"They're a lively lot. Yes, I had fun but... I think Alice and Linda have their eye on Bert. It felt a little awkward. Also, he looked a little tired. So, I thought I'd ease off."

Abby had noticed their name tags but she couldn't recall which name belonged to which woman. "What about the other women? Are they making eyes at Bert too?"

"I think they'd like to. They're probably waiting for an opportunity to get a word in edgewise. Alice and Linda are quite chatty. Anyhow, where are we going?"

"I'm famished and craving a steak or a second breakfast. I haven't decided which one I want more yet. I'm headed back to town. Now that you're here, I thought I could give you a bit of a tour. Oh, look... We're coming up to the lake where we had the picnic a short while ago."

"The lake where you found a dead body?" her mom asked.

Abby bit the edge of her lip. "You can see there are farmhouses dotting the countryside. Some are close to the road with the paddocks undulating into the distance. And here's the farmhouse where I..." Abby broke off and sighed. The farmhouse where she'd cornered a person of interest. In fact, the woman had been a killer and Abby had come close to meeting an unhappy end. "Isn't the countryside pretty, Mom? I love driving out early in the morning. Sometimes, the mist hangs low over the hills and makes everything look haunted."

"An ideal destination for ghosts," her mom mused.

Abby looked down at Doyle in time to see his worried expression. "I'm sinking here, Doyle," she mouthed.

"Oh, can we drop by the antique store?" her mom asked. "I want to meet Joyce's fiancé properly. You rarely talk about him. I've seen him from a distance but I've never had the chance to have a proper chat with him."

"He's not exactly the chatty type, Mom." Abby sank into her seat. Bradford Mills didn't like people going into his antique store. While he opened the store every day, he enjoyed settling down at his counter to read and write... in peace and quiet.

"I seem to remember you saying he'd worked as a newspaper reporter."

"Yes. He's writing a book now, but he doesn't like to talk about it. I think it's a thriller."

"With all the incidents taking place in this town," her mom said, "you'd think he'd be inspired to write a murder mystery."

"So, did Bert ignore you?" Abby asked as she tried to change the subject.

"Oh, no. We had a lovely chat. He showed a lot of interest in my job saying that as an accountant he'd always envied people who could spend their days doing something fun and creative like drawing. I thought he was being polite but then he told me his wife used to love hunting down original book illustrations. You'll never guess, so I'll tell you. He told me he'd put all his wife's belongings in storage and he remembered seeing a drawing of a rabbit. I asked him about it and I'm sure it's a Beatrix Potter drawing of Peter Rabbit."

"Wow. That must be worth quite a bit."

"That's what I told him. He actually offered to send it to me."

"Double wow."

"Exactly. I made it clear I couldn't possibly accept such a gift but he insisted. Even after I told him he could sell it for a profit. He said he had more money than he knew what to do with. He's quite a gentleman and made sure to always include me in the conversation." Her mom sighed. "A couple of times, someone dropped a serviette on top of the cell phone. I'm sure they did it by accident. Anyhow, Bert acted promptly and removed it."

"Does he have family?"

"Yes, a son and a daughter. He's been a widower for a number of years."

"And he's picking up the tab for this trip?" That struck Abby as odd. People could be generous… Up to a point.

"He mentioned something about his kids doing quite well. I'm sure he gave them something. Or maybe he put some money aside for the grandkids. His daughter has two children but his son is still single."

"He must have won a large amount to be able to afford such a trip," Abby mused.

"Yes, I suppose. He said they're traveling right around the country. Most tourists stick to the main cities, but he wanted to do a thorough tour of out of the way places."

When they reached Eden, Abby pulled up outside the antique store, Brilliant Baubles. She could see Bradford Mills standing behind the counter. Hard to miss him, she thought, as he always wore a khaki shirt and hunting jacket with a variety of pens poking out of his pocket.

"How about we look at the window display first?" Abby suggested. From experience, she knew she needed to play it safe by getting the lay of the land first. At some point, she expected Bradford would look up. When he did, she hoped she'd be able to pick up on his mood. Although, his deadpan expression sometimes made it difficult to gauge how he felt.

"If he doesn't like customers coming into his store, why did he go into business?" her mom asked.

Abby scratched around her mind for an answer. "From memory, he inherited the store. When he came to check it out, he decided to stay on. His uncle had been well known in the area and he wanted to keep his memory alive."

Her mom sighed. "And now he's engaged to Joyce. So, he found happiness."

Yes, Abby thought, there's still hope. Her mom had never pushed her to settle down but she knew she'd be happier if her only daughter found someone special to share her life with.

"Oh, look," her mom exclaimed. "He has books. They look like first editions. Let's go in."

Abby exchanged a worried look with Doyle. The moment she stepped inside the store, she felt Bradford lifting his gaze toward her. She gave him a tentative smile and waved her cell phone.

"Eleanor," he said and surprised Abby by sauntering toward them. "I heard you were in town. Welcome to Eden."

"Oh, is that an illustrated Enid Blyton? Abby, The Faraway Tree was always your favorite."

Abby wondered if they'd need white gloves to handle the book. Before she could decide what to do, Bradford picked up the book. As he turned the pages to show her mom, they heard the blaring sound of a car horn.

No, Abby thought, not a car horn…

Turning, Abby saw the tourist bus speeding by.

"What was that?" her mom asked.

"I'm… I'm not sure." Abby frowned. Handing over the cell phone to Bradford, she strode toward the front door and peered down the street just as the tourist bus turned into the corner, the wheels screeching when it came to a sudden stop.

Looking over her shoulder, she mouthed, "I'll be back."

Doyle jumped to his feet, looked from Abby to Bradford and scurried toward Abby. They trotted down the street. Along the way, she saw people hurrying their steps toward the pub while others were only now emerging from the stores. Joyce erupted from the café and nearly crashed into her.

"What's going on?" Joyce asked. "Oh, hello. I heard

you were back, Abby." Joyce gave her a lifted eyebrow look. "You haven't come in for a coffee."

"I was about to." Abby picked up her pace and Joyce kept up with her. Looking down the street she saw the tourist bus had stopped at an angle outside the pub.

"This doesn't look good," Joyce said. "I heard your mom joined the tourist group. I hope she's all right."

Abby spent a second wondering how Joyce had heard the news about her mom so quickly and then gave up. Clearly, the Eden grapevine continued to broadcast loud and clear. "Um, you know she's not really here."

Shrugging, Joyce said, "Faith told us we need to pretend she is here."

Just before they reached the corner, Abby pulled Joyce back. "Is that the ambulance I hear?"

Joyce pressed her hand to her chest. "I don't like the look of this."

The tourists had piled out of the bus and were standing by on the sidewalk. Some of the women had their hands pressed against their cheeks. She counted three... four men standing by and shaking their heads.

Mitch and Markus emerged from the pub. After taking in the scene, they tried to coax people inside the pub.

Most went in, but they did so looking over their shoulders.

"We should stay here and give them space to do what they have to do," Abby said.

Joyce agreed with a slow nod. "Maybe someone had

an attack. I hope it's nothing serious." She wrung her hands. "They all looked so happy when they came in this morning to get coffee for their trip."

Aha! So that's how she knew about her mom joining the group…

Doyle whimpered.

"I bet Doyle knows what's going on," Joyce mused. "Dogs are extremely sensitive. They sense things that we can't even see or hear."

Abby picked him up and, tucking his little head under her chin, she held him close to her chest.

As the ambulance approached, the siren stopped blaring but the red and blue lights remained on, shining brightly against the gray sky. Everyone who'd come out to see what had happened stood by in silence.

"I'm guessing it's a man," Abby said under her breath.

"Why?" Joyce asked.

"Most of the people who went inside the pub are women. They're all standing by the windows looking out." She trawled through her mind trying to remember how many women she'd seen in the group. "If I had my cell phone, I'd be able to tell you for sure. I took a photo of the group earlier on."

"Where is your phone?"

"I left it with Bradford."

"Should I ask?"

Abby rolled her eyes as she explained about her mom wanting to browse through the antique store. "The tourist bus sped by, honking its horn. Yeah, I really didn't like the sound of that. The less my mom knows about this, the better."

"You're going to keep her in the dark? She's going to find out."

Abby shook her head. "Not until I have more information. I don't want her to worry." Studying the crowd standing near the bus, Abby tried to read their expressions as they watched the ambulance officers hard at work.

If they crossed the street, they'd get a better view but that felt too ghoulish. "I should head back to the store and check on my mom."

"I think you should tell her," Joyce murmured. "Honesty is always the best policy."

"Tell her what? We don't know anything yet. No point in worrying her." Even as she spoke, she tried to remember the people who'd been herded inside the pub. She'd seen several women and a couple of men. There were other people standing on the other side of the bus so Abby couldn't do a full head count. She supposed she'd find out soon enough.

~

When Abby returned to Brilliant Baubles she found Bradford kneeling down in front of a chest aiming the cell phone down, presumably so Abby's mom could see inside as he drew out one book and then another.

"This is a treasure trove," her mom exclaimed. "I haven't seen picture books like these in ages. Add that one too. What's the one underneath the blue one? That looks interesting."

Bradford looked up but his expression gave nothing away.

Abby didn't see any need to raise the alarm, so she refrained from mentioning anything about the tour bus or the ambulance.

Looking at the pile of books Bradford had set aside, Abby said, "Oh, my mom will love these. She collects illustrated books."

"Yes, she's been telling me," he murmured.

Bradford, bless his soul, appeared to be exercising the patience of an oyster. Abby had heard say he'd been known to ask browsers to go away and come back when they knew exactly what they wanted.

"No, not that one," her mom said. "The next one. Yes, that's it. Let me see inside. No, it's not what I thought it would be. Try the next one."

"I'll take over," Abby offered. "Thanks, Bradford."

He took his time getting up, which made Abby wonder if he'd actually been enjoying himself.

"Make sure to put those books we selected aside for me, please. Abby will pay for them. She can bring them over next time she comes to visit."

"Or, you could collect them when you come to visit me." Abby swapped places with Bradford and followed her mom's instructions.

"This is better than on-line shopping. Someone should set themselves up to do this for people who don't like the trouble of going into stores," her mom said and added, "where did you get to?"

"Huh?"

"You stepped out. Where did you go?"

"You know me. I'm a curious bunny. A bunch of hooligans raced along the main street," she fibbed. "Everyone came out to see. They'll be talking about it all day. We can't have this sort of behavior. Someone will no doubt bring that up at the next town meeting." Abby tried to distract her mom with another book and when that didn't work, she got up and walked around the store.

"I think I've seen enough for today," her mom said. "There's so much to see here, I want to come and look around with a fresh set of eyes. Didn't you say you were going to have lunch at the pub?"

"Maybe I'll grab a bite at the café. I... I bumped into Joyce and told her I'd be swinging by for a coffee." She turned and waved to Bradford. While she didn't expect a response from him, she noticed the edge of his lip lifted ever so slightly.

"Abby. I'm looking at the pavement. You'll have to hold the cell phone up."

Looking down the street, Abby noticed the ambulance had already left.

"Oh, what's going on out here?" her mom asked. "Where did all these people come from?"

News must have spread fast. Abby couldn't remember ever seeing so many people out and about. "I guess it's that time of day. We get a lot of farmers coming into town at about this time." As a gust of wind swept around her, Abby pulled up her collar. "I'm still in sunny weather mode but I'm glad I remembered to grab my jacket." Doyle looked up at her and gave her a doggy grin. "I think Doyle needs to start wearing his little tartan jacket. Wait until you see it, Mom. It's adorable."

"I meant to say, I'd been feeling awkward dressed in a T-shirt while everyone else in the group wore proper winter attire. So, I set the air-conditioner on high and put on a sweater. Someone mentioned it might snow soon but it won't be as much as you get up on the ski slopes."

Seeing the tourist bus making a turn to park properly, Abby hurried her step and ducked inside the café. She needed news about the incident but had to be careful her mom didn't overhear.

If only lady luck would smile upon her and bring down the wi-fi and play havoc with the roaming signal. Her finger inched toward the off switch, but she couldn't bring herself to do it. Joyce had several flower vases displayed on side tables. As she strode by one, she considered dropping her cell phone into one of them but then she remembered it was water resistant...

"Table for two?" Joyce asked getting right into the

spirit of the game. "Hello, Eleanor. So good to see you again."

"You're looking lovely, Joyce." Her mom admired Joyce's short bob. "You do the Audrey Hepburn look very well."

"Thank you." Joyce signaled with her eyes.

Abby frowned. She could interpret raised eyebrows, but she couldn't quite figure out what Joyce wanted to say. Did she want Abby to follow her? Drawing out a chair, she made sure to sit facing the street so her mom would be facing the other way. Once she settled down, Joyce positioned herself so Abby's mom couldn't see her and she proceeded to make hand gestures.

Joyce joined her hands as if praying and looked heavenward.

Yes, Abby thought, she too prayed the person had come through all right. Abby smiled and nodded.

That prompted Joyce to frown at her and shake her head. She then crossed her hands over her chest and closed her eyes. After a moment, she puffed up her cheeks and appeared to make an attempt to play an instrument.

Abby had never been much good at charades.

"Well? Are you going to order?" her mom asked.

"Oh, yes. I'm waiting for Joyce to come back. She's... off with the fairies today."

"I recommend the Heavenly Pancakes," Joyce said. "They're good enough to make any angel smile and play the harp."

Huh?

Joyce strode around the table and leaned down to look at the cell phone. "Eleanor, do you think angels play harps in heaven?"

"I don't know dear. I rather hope we get to choose what we listen to. I'm partial to a bit of The Grateful Dead."

Straightening, Joyce scribbled something on her order book and held it up for Abby to see.

Dead?

"Who?" Abby mouthed.

"I'd hate to say this about your fine establishment, Joyce," her mom murmured, "but everyone looks a little downcast."

"Oh, the weather tends to have that effect, Eleanor. If it's not the heat, it's the cold," Joyce said and mouthed, "Dead." She held up her order book again.

Abby gasped as she read the name.

Chapter Three

*a*bby switched seats and repositioned her cell phone to face the street. "I'll be back in a moment, Mom." She strode over to the counter, her eyes wide as she stared at Joyce. "Dead?" she whispered.

Joyce nodded. "I don't have all the details yet. One of the girls just came in for her shift and she said she saw the ambulance officer covering the body with a sheet. That sounds quite final to me, and she also heard someone giving his name to the police officer."

Abby nearly choked on the words, "The police came?"

Joyce shrugged. "I believe they're still there. I didn't see any police cars drive by so they must have come in from the opposite direction."

Abby looked over at her table and, shaking her head, said, "My mom can't find out about this. Not just yet.

Spread the word around. Whatever happens, no one is allowed to mention his name. Understood?"

Joyce turned to her waitresses. "Everyone. Battle stations. Attend to each table and pass on the message." Turning back to Abby, she smiled. "See, all taken care of."

"People are so friendly," her mom said when Abby returned to her table. "I've been watching them stroll by and stop for a chat. Everyone seems to know everyone."

"Yes, it's a friendly town." Abby looked around her and noticed people at nearby tables glancing her way and nodding. A couple of people even gave her a thumbs up sign.

"So, what did you decide to get?" her mom asked.

"The full breakfast. Joyce serves it all day." Abby had no idea how she'd fit it in. Her hunger had come and gone... "I'm still adjusting to the time difference." If anything, Abby thought, a full breakfast would keep her at the café for a while. "Excuse me. I... I need to use the restroom."

Abby rushed up to the counter again. "I need you to get word to Mitch and Markus. Tell them to get everyone at the pub up to speed," she told Joyce. "There's to be no mention of the incident, not within my mom's hearing. Understood?"

Joyce gave her a tight smile. "I didn't realize you could be so bossy. I like it but it doesn't really suit you. Perhaps with some practice..."

Abby flapped her arms. "Can we focus, please. I just

told my mom I'm having the full breakfast. Keep the food coming. I want to stay here for as long as possible." Out of sight, out of mind, she thought. Hopefully, by the time she returned to the pub, everyone would be on the same page and acting as if nothing had happened.

"Are you sure you're up to the task of misleading your mom?" Joyce asked. "You don't strike me as the type. In fact, I bet you were a girl scout. You probably turn beetroot red when you fib."

"If I don't try, I'll never be able to convince her to come down for a visit. I only need some thinking time to figure out how to break the news to her. People die all the time. This shouldn't really count. She's convinced this town is not safe."

Joyce gave her a pat on the shoulder. "Don't worry. We've got your back. News about your ruse is spreading like wildfire. In a strange way, this is softening the blow and taking everyone's mind off what happened. You're doing the town a service. Keep up the good work. I'll call Mitch straightaway."

Abby thanked her and swung back toward her table.

Of all the things that could have happened, why did someone have to go and die today… of all days? Here, in her idyllic little town.

She looked up in time to see Faith coming to a screeching halt outside the café and plastering her face against the window, her eyes frantic as she scanned the tables. When she spotted her, she gave Abby a vigorous wave.

"Did anyone think to contact Faith?" Abby asked under her breath. Abby made a few hand gestures, but Faith's puzzled expression suggested none of it had made sense. Finally, Abby clamped her hand over her mouth and then made a slashing gesture against her throat. A clear message, she thought, to avoid talking about the death.

Faith jumped back from the window, looked to one side and then the other and then back at Abby.

Abby groaned. "Okay, maybe she misunderstood that message and now thinks I want to kill her."

Just as Faith made a move to come into the café, Joyce rushed out and grabbed her.

"I need to get myself another cell phone," Abby said under her breath as she sat down.

"What's going on with Faith?" her mom asked. "And why is Joyce shaking her?"

"Joyce can be… overly dramatic," Abby said. "Oh, look. Here comes my breakfast."

"Faith looks surprised now. Whatever Joyce told her must have come as a shock. Hang on. Now she's laughing."

"Yum. Can you believe this breakfast?" Abby exclaimed.

"It's lunchtime, sweetie. Actually, that does look scrumptious. I swear, by the time I get back home, I will have gained several pounds. I never knew traveling around would make me so hungry."

Abby frowned but decided not to say anything to

contradict her mom. She managed to get two bites in before Faith approached her table.

Faith appeared to be struggling to keep a straight face as she said, "Hello. How's your jet lag?"

"Fine. Doyle woke me up," Abby said around a mouthful of bacon. "Now he's snoozing. Again."

Faith leaned over the table and waved to Eleanor. "How are you enjoying your virtual trip?"

Abby switched off the conversation and tried to figure out how she'd break the news. Her mom had never been a crier, but Abby felt she should have someone with her when she told her about the unfortunate death.

She considered contacting one of her neighbors. Lou-Anne Fellows had retired early from teaching and enjoyed spending her days in her pottery studio out the back. A couple of times a week, she dropped by for a coffee. The other neighbor gave piano lessons every afternoon but dropped in to have a chat in the morning. Checking the time and working out the difference, Abby decided Lou-Anne would be her best bet, but she'd have to wait until she got back to the pub so she could look up the phone number. Abby gave a firm nod and decided that's what she'd do. Yes, she would organize Lou-Anne and make sure she could be nearby when Abby gave her mom the news.

"I was just telling your mom it's been a really quiet day at the newspaper." Faith quirked her eyebrows up. "I can't decide if it's a no news day or a slow news day. I think I'm going with a slow news day."

Abby guessed Faith wanted her to give her a prompt. What to say and when.

"I'm happy to have a no news day." Abby nodded. "I'm still in vacation mode and I'd like to keep it that way for a while."

Faith nodded. "Okay, I'll go along with that, but you know what they say about Murphy's Law..." Faith rose to her feet saying she needed to get back to the office in case some news came in and ruined their no-news-day.

Abby turned her attention back to her breakfast and focused on pacing herself. When she reached the halfway point, Joyce appeared and set a plate of pancakes down on the table.

"I hope you can fit these in." Joyce quirked her eyebrows up and down. The affliction seemed to be spreading. "My heart breaks to see good food go to waste," Joyce said and pressed her fisted hand against her heart a couple of times.

It took Abby a moment to realize Joyce was trying to pass on a message.

"Then again, too much food can be detrimental to your health. Especially fatty food." Joyce's eyebrows danced up and down again.

Abby eyed the sausage on her plate and then it hit her.

Heart attack?

"I'm inclined to agree with Joyce," her mom

murmured. "Abby, are you sure you need that much food?"

"I didn't eat on the plane. I'm sure Doyle will take me on enough walks to burn it all off." Abby finished her savory meal and started working her way through the pancakes, one nibble at a time. She could do this. She knew she could.

An hour later, she managed to push the last bite in.

"Well, if I hadn't seen it with my own eyes, I would not have believed it." Her mom laughed. "I don't remember you ever having such a healthy appetite at home. The meals at Joyce's must be scrumptious."

"They certainly are." Trying to be as discreet as possible, Abby loosened her belt.

"So, what now?" her mom chirped.

"You know what they say about eating on the run. I think I should sit back and digest my meal first."

"I believe the warning is about swimming after eating. A walk would do you good," her mom suggested.

Abby shook her head. "I'm sure the warning also applies to walking. I remember reading something about it for one of my articles. Exercise diverts blood flow from the digestive system and there's a risk of stomach cramps because blood and oxygen are redirected to the muscles from the digestive process."

Her mom chortled, "You're making that up."

"Am not. Look it up." Knowing her mom wouldn't stop badgering her, Abby stood up. Baby steps, she thought. "I'll just go pay for all this." Although, she had the feeling she'd be paying for it with more than money.

~

"Are we headed in the right direction?" her mom asked.

"I'm following Doyle and he seems to want to go this way," Abby said as they headed away from the pub. The longer she stayed away, the better her chances of avoiding the tourist group…

"If Doyle is leading you this way, shouldn't he be in front of you?"

Abby peered over her shoulder. Doyle was lagging behind and looking over his shoulder, probably thinking about his special spot by the lovely fireplace at the pub. "He was in front of me a moment ago, now he's sniffing something. That's what dogs do, Mom. Come on, Doyle. Keep up."

Doyle scurried on ahead, stopped outside a store and looked at Abby.

When Abby reached the store, she looked in the window. "I've been meaning to get a new pair of jeans. Maybe I should go in and have a look around." And kill some more time, she thought, trying to delay her return to the pub for as long as possible.

"Do you think this is the best time for it, Abby? You've just pigged out. You'd have to shoehorn yourself into them."

Abby smiled. "Thanks for the motherly advice. More reason to keep walking."

Doyle sighed and hung his head as if to say he had no reason for the extra exercise because he hadn't pigged out.

"Here comes trouble," her mom exclaimed.

Abby looked up and saw Detective Joshua Ryan headed her way. When he saw her, he stopped and ducked inside a store.

"That looked odd. I get the feeling he's trying to avoid you, Abby."

Abby guessed he wanted to avoid being seen by her mom. Too late, she thought, knowing very little escaped her mom's attention. "Why would he do that? We get along great."

"Oh, do you? Tell me more."

"Mom, you've never been a matchmaker. Please don't start now."

"You said it yourself, you get along. That's a solid foundation."

"For friendship," Abby clarified.

As they strode past the store, Joshua waved to her. Abby kept the phone pointed in the opposite direction and mouthed, "What?"

Joshua wrote something down on his notebook and held it up.

Why did he want to meet?

Nodding, she continued along her way. When she

turned the corner, she peered over her shoulder and saw Joshua following several steps behind.

Had she set something into motion?

—◌—

"This is the residents' entrance to the pub," Abby said. "I usually come in this way to avoid being distracted when I just want to get to my apartment." Or, she thought, when she wanted to keep her mom in the dark...

Abby took the stairs two steps at a time and hoped she wouldn't bump into any of the tourists along the way. "You must be getting sleepy."

Right on cue, her mom yawned. "I'm trying to adjust to your time but I think it might take a couple of days. If you don't mind, I'm going to take a quick nap."

Striding into her apartment, Abby nearly collapsed with relief. "You go ahead and do that."

"I should be awake in time for dinnertime," her mom said. "I wouldn't mind catching up with the group."

One hurdle at a time, Abby thought. "Okay. You call me when you're ready and I'll set up the video chat again."

She sank into the couch and groaned. "Doyle, if you could talk I'm sure you'd have a few choice words to say about human behavior. What was I supposed to do?"

She sent Joshua a text message. A few minutes later, he knocked on her door.

Abby smiled. "Come in at your own peril. I might be contagious."

Joshua chuckled and looked at her cell phone.

Abby nodded. "It's safe to talk. My mom's taking a break."

He sighed. "I don't know how you did it, but you managed to organize an entire town to do your bidding. Everyone is speaking in hushed tones and looking over their shoulders to make sure you're nowhere near them."

"Well, I've been here long enough to know they're going along because they know I'm going to fall on my face at some point. This will backfire on me, I'm sure it will, and the good folk of Eden just love the entertainment factor, especially on a slow news day. Please tell me this is one of them."

"Looks like it," Joshua said.

"So, what are you doing in town?"

"A tourist dying while on vacation?" He slumped down on the couch. "It's usually up to the police to notify the next of kin."

"Oh. I see. That must be tough."

"Yeah," he raked his fingers through his hair. "It's the grim side of the job. The relatives live in Melbourne so the local police had to take care of it." He looked around. "I don't suppose you have a drink here."

Abby strode over to her tiny kitchen and dug out a bottle of wine and a couple of glasses. "Wine?"

He checked his watch. "That'll do. I'm officially off-duty."

"So, what happened?" Abby hadn't had any time to think about the events that had ended with a tourist dead outside the pub. She had gaps and her natural curiosity needed them to be filled.

"The bus driver made a call to emergency services saying someone on the bus appeared to be having a heart attack," Joshua explained. "He asked the operator where the ambulance would be coming from. Rather than stopping the bus, he decided to meet them half way and so he drove into town."

Abby gave a pensive nod. "Oh, yes. I think he tried to clear the way by tooting his horn. That's when we noticed the bus cannoning into town." Abby brushed her hand across her face. She too had been thinking on her feet. In that split second, Abby had decided to bide her time and withhold the information from her mom for as long as possible. Had it been the right decision?

"Despite the bus driver's efforts, he didn't make it in time." Joshua took a sip of wine and then pushed out a breath. "So, what's this about you keeping your mom out of the loop?"

Abby sat down and tucked her feet under her. "Yeah, it wasn't one of my brightest ideas. I'm afraid I fell victim to my own knee jerk reaction. Mom's so reluctant to travel, I didn't want her to think about the risks she could face." She leaned back and groaned. "I cannot believe this."

"Yeah, how dare he die while you're trying to impress your mom."

"Go ahead. Have fun at my expense."

"So, what's the plan?" Joshua asked. "You can't possibly keep this from her. She's bound to notice someone missing from the group."

Nibbling the tip of her thumb, she shrugged. "I'll have to find the appropriate moment to break it to her. That reminds me, I have to make a call." She searched through her contact list and found the number for her mom's neighbor. When she finished the call, she poured herself another glass of wine. "Lou-Anne is level-headed and knows how jittery my mom is about traveling. She'll be at hand when I decide to come clean." A load off her mind, Abby thought.

"Do you actually think your mom will be upset?"

Abby gave a small shrug. "Despite her strange aversion to traveling, Mom is level-headed too." She brushed her hand across her forehead. "After dad died, she brought me up alone and did such a good job, I never felt I was missing out on anything. Our lives had been shattered and my life could have been shadowed by the loss but mom filled each day with brightness. I don't know what to think at this point. I know she's strong. Regardless, I can't help thinking this is bad news and she shouldn't be alone when I break it to her. I'm sure I would have done the same for anyone else."

Doyle clambered up onto the couch and curled up on her lap.

"Did he have a pre-existing condition?" Abby asked.

"There will most likely be an autopsy so we'll have to wait for the results."

Abby wondered if there had been any warning signs. "He looked fit and healthy."

"Stress can be a killer," Joshua mused.

Abby frowned. "While on vacation? I don't think so."

"Who knows? He might have forgotten to take his medication."

"What's everyone in town saying?" Abby asked. "I've been with Mom for most of the day so I haven't had a chance to talk with anyone else."

"They're mostly talking about his age. The usual stuff. Too young to die. They have a point. You work all your life. Then you retire and you think you're finally enjoying life when it's suddenly cut short."

They both sipped their wines in silence for a few minutes.

"You just never know when it's all going to end."

Abby agreed. "It serves as a reminder to always make the best of it and never leave for tomorrow what you can do today."

"That reminds me…" Joshua finished his drink and checked his watch. "I have one more thing to do before I head on home. The pathologist wants a list of his medication or the actual meds. He assumes he'd been taking something."

Abby had no idea what compelled her to follow Joshua. He sent Mitch a text and within a few minutes Mitch came up with the room key.

While Mitch stood by the door, Joshua dug inside his pocket and produced some rubber gloves.

"Really?" Abby asked. She didn't have any business going inside, so she remained by the door.

"Habit," he said. "Also, it pays to play it safe." Joshua did a thorough search through the room looking for all the meds.

He found a bottle on the bedside table and another two in the toiletries bag.

"Okay. All done here."

"What about his personal effects?" Abby asked.

"I organized another officer to come tomorrow and collect everything, but his daughter insisted on doing it herself."

Really? Joshua had said she lived in Melbourne. She'd have to drive for over three hours. "You'd think she'd want to avoid making such a trip so soon after hearing about her loss."

Joshua shrugged. "She's determined. The police officer I spoke with said she came across as the type who enjoys being super organized and in control."

"That's a blessing in disguise," Abby said. "At least he didn't have to deal with someone in shock."

Joshua looked pensive. "Shock. Disbelief. Denial.

Hysterics. I've seen it all. I'm just glad I didn't have to tell her myself. You'd think I'd be used to it by now, but it always leaves me slightly shaken. Sometimes I think a part of me crumbles a little... Who knows? Maybe it does, but I..."

"But you soldier on."

"Yeah. You have to."

When Joshua finished his search, he gave a firm nod and stepped out of the room.

"He kept a tidy room," Abby couldn't help saying as a feeling of awkwardness swept through her. A person's life had ended and suddenly, everything that had been private became public.

Mitch locked the door and asked, "Will you be coming down?"

"Yes, later on. My mom's taking a nap."

"Traveling can be exhausting." Mitch nodded. "Give me a heads up when you decide to come down. I might have to remind everyone to steer clear of the subject. It's all everyone can talk about."

"What about the tourists?" Abby asked. "Have they been out and about?"

Mitch shook his head. "No. They've kept to themselves. One of the women took it really hard and had to be sedated." Shrugging, Mitch went back down to the bar.

Joshua held up the bag of medication. "I should deliver these to the pathologist. I'll see you around, Abby."

Returning to her apartment, Abby couldn't shake off the feeling of death lurking nearby. A man who'd died had been staying in a room two doors down from where she slept. If he hadn't had the heart attack out on the road, he might have died in his sleep or in the pub.

Hearing her cell phone ringing, she hurried her step and answered on the last ring. "Faith. What's up?"

"How did I do today? I hope I didn't give anything away. I'm worried I might have put my foot in it."

"Relax. You did great."

"Relax? I thought you were cross with me."

"Oh, yeah. The slash your throat motion." Abby chuckled. "You did well. My mom doesn't suspect anything." She stretched out on the couch with Doyle at her feet. "I can't believe the day I've had and now I'm having the strangest thoughts. Serves me right. I should have stayed put. It felt strange going into a room previously occupied by someone who is now dead."

"You'd think you'd be immune to it all," Faith said.

"No. It's all so final…" Looking up at the ceiling, Abby remembered waking up that morning on the couch.

Abby sprung upright as she recalled a stray thought she'd had that morning. "Last night, on my way up, I felt really out of it and I think I might have tried to go into the wrong room."

"Without a key?" Faith asked.

Abby scratched around her mind. "I only had a

couple of beers but after my three-hour drive and the long flight over before that, I felt exhausted."

"You had three beers."

"Fine. Three beers. Anyhow, I remember apologizing to someone. They opened the door just as I was about to insert the key."

"What did they say?"

Abby tried to remember. "Nothing. When they saw me at the door, they closed it again."

"That's odd. You'd think they would have said something or... come out. Why did they open the door?"

"Maybe they heard me trying to open it." Tapping her chin, Abby remembered having the key in her hand. Doyle had led the way and...

Yes, she'd been tired from all the traveling. She must have been really out of it to try to open the wrong door or maybe she'd been distracted. She would have asked her mom, but after waving goodnight to the tourist group, her mom had said she needed to get some shut-eye so she could get up at the same time as Abby.

"What's going through your mind?" Faith asked.

"Now? I have no idea." Yes, she had been distracted. "Last night, I'd been thinking about the tourist group staying at the pub. I haven't been here long enough to see the pub in full swing. I know it gets busier during the skiing season..." Yes, she'd been thinking about that as she'd made her way to her apartment. Maybe that's why she'd ended up trying to open the wrong door.

Three beers were not enough to kill all her brain cells. Needing to prove the point, she searched through everything she could remember from the previous night.

When Abby had decided to call it a night, her mom had insisted she hold the phone up so she could say goodnight to everyone in the group.

Yes, they'd all been at the bar. Or had they? She closed her eyes and tried to picture their faces. Had Steph been with the group? What about Alice and Linda?

Abby shook her head. "Here's a stray thought... I think one of the women had been in his room and... I think he might have been having a fling."

Abby sank back down on the couch. "Being sneaky is hard work. Mom will expect me to go down to the bar tonight. I don't know how long I can keep this up without falling on my face."

"Do you want me to come to the pub?" Faith asked.

"Yes, please. I could do with the extra support. I'll see you in a couple of hours."

Doyle stirred and yawned.

Giving him a scratch under the chin, Abby asked, "Did I feed you today? Sorry, Doyle. I'm in a bit of a daze." She changed the water in his bowl and opened a can of his favorite food. "While you have your dinner, I'm going to freshen up and see if I can find a loose pair of jeans."

Chapter Four

"*How* was your sleep, Mom?"

"Great. I dozed off in my armchair. I think it sort of gave me an authentic feeling of dozing off in a bus. Oh, and I checked my inbox. Would you believe it? Bert sent me an email asking for my address so he can post the Beatrix Potter drawing. I felt awkward for about a minute and then I got over it. It's going to take pride of place in my study. I suggested the postage might cost less if he sent it to you. I guess I'll have to wait to hear back from him. Anyway, I'm all set for the rest of the night. When we go downstairs to the bar, pan the cell phone around. I want to see what you see when you go down."

Abby took a moment to make sure she didn't walk out looking like roadkill. "Come on, Doyle. It's happy hour."

Doyle scurried on ahead and made a beeline for the

fireplace. Abby scanned the bar and then panned the cell phone, her time delay, she thought pleased to see everyone going about their business as usual.

Or so she thought.

Someone noticed her and nudged the person next to them. That set off a domino effect. Within a few minutes, everyone in the bar looked her way and waved, the smiles on their faces not quite matching their worried expressions.

The waitresses had stopped in mid-stride as if waiting for a prompt from Abby. Even Mitch froze in place.

Abby made a rolling motion with her hand.

"What just happened?" her mom asked.

Abby grinned. "I have no idea. After several months of living in this town, I have decided to just go with the flow and not ask too many questions."

"I don't see the tourist group anywhere. Could you go into the dining room, Abby? I'd like to find out how the rest of their day trip turned out."

Panicking, Abby dug deep for a distraction. "Oh, look. Here's Markus sitting on his comfy chair by the fireplace. Say hello, Markus. He actually mentioned wanting to give you a guided tour of all the photographs in the pub. There's quite a lot of history here, Mom. I think you'd enjoy it." Abby didn't give her mom or Markus time to object. Handing the cell phone over, she backed away and sank into a barstool.

Mitch leaned forward and whispered, "You haven't told her yet."

Abby shook her head. "You know me well enough by now. I'm not the type of person to say this, but I need a drink."

Mitch wagged a finger at her. "You've made it too complicated. I've had some people say they're afraid of putting a foot wrong and think they should stay away but they don't dare because they're afraid they'll miss out on you putting a foot wrong."

That didn't surprise Abby. "Hey, do you remember the tourist group coming into the bar last night?"

He nodded. "They had a late dinner and then finished up here. Why?"

His last meal. His last drink with friends...

"Just checking to make sure I hadn't imagined it." Abby looked around the bar. There were several small tables and a long table at one end everyone referred to as the captain's table and that's where the tourist group had settled in. "Do you remember seeing any of them going upstairs during the evening?"

Mitch straightened and wiped the counter. "Are you chasing a story, Abby?"

"I might be, but it's only gossip." The more she thought about it, the more she felt it had been odd for the person to close the door without saying anything. If they'd opened the door in response to Abby trying to fit her key in, then it would have made sense for them to say something.

That didn't sound right. Now that she thought about it, they'd actually opened the door before she'd tried to fit the key in. Meaning... What? They'd been on their way out and hadn't wanted to be seen leaving the room?

She took a sip of her drink and shrugged. "Never mind. I'm only trying to get back into the swing of things." And find out who'd been having an affair, Abby thought.

"By asking pointless questions?" Mitch asked. "That doesn't make sense unless you think someone's up to something."

Abby straightened and grinned. "I'm a student of human nature and like to know why people behave the way they do." She swung around on her barstool. Markus stood at one end of the bar and appeared to be doing a methodical job of explaining each photo to her mom. The walls were covered with them, some dating back to the 1800s. She'd definitely put her mom in safe hands.

"If you're looking for the tourists, they're in the dining room," Mitch said.

"All of them?"

"All except one. She ordered room service and said she still felt too upset to join the others." Mitch clicked his fingers. "Cynthia."

Abby brought up a mental image of the woman, matching the name to the face.

"She had the local doctor attend to her," Mitch

added. "Apparently, her blood pressure dropped from the shock."

"I suppose that's normal behavior. They're all friends. Abby shivered. She hoped her mom didn't take it too hard. "I keep forgetting it's winter here. I'm going to have to go upstairs and get a sweater. If Faith comes in, tell her I'll be down in a sec." Along the way, she wondered if Cynthia had been the one she'd seen when she'd tried to open the wrong door.

The rooms at the pub were all on the first floor. Being at the end of the hallway afforded Abby some privacy, or so she assumed. She hadn't tested the theory yet. Once the skiing season kicked in, she'd been told the place would fill up and, she guessed, that meant there would be more noise with people coming and going at all hours.

Finding the sweater she wanted, she strode out again. Along the way, she heard a murmured conversation coming from one of the rooms.

None of your business, Abby. Just keeping walking, she told herself.

When she settled back at the bar, Mitch lifted his eyebrows and gestured to the other end of the bar.

"You'll have to tell me how you talked Markus into holding your mom hostage."

She hadn't exactly asked. Maybe she had become bossy. As she swirled around to check on them, she saw Joyce and Bradford coming into the pub.

Mitch grinned. "No one wants to miss the action. This is good for business."

Abby swung back and stared into space.

Frowning, Mitch said, "You look lost in thought."

"I'm trying to snatch a bit of quiet time."

"At the pub?"

Abby made a sweeping gesture with her hand. "I'm okay, so long as I let the noise wash over me. Once this is over, I'm going to need a vacation."

"Um, don't panic just yet. Markus is back in his chair by the fireplace but your mom, a.k.a. your cell phone, is not with him."

"What?" Abby jumped off her barstool and rushed toward Markus. "What have you done with my mom?"

"Relax. She's having dinner with Joyce and Bradford."

"But I gave you clear instructions."

Markus shrugged. "There's only so much I can say about my ancestors. I tried to paint a rosy picture but, to be honest with you, I'm sure half of them were scoundrels and I don't like to lie."

Abby rushed off toward the dining room and nearly crashed into a waitress. Everyone in town had come in for dinner and they all now turned to look at her. Some made discreet gestures toward the table in the middle of the dining room. That's where she found Joyce and Bradford with her mom, the cell phone propped against a wine bottle.

Only two tables away from the tourist group. What had they been thinking?

She reached the table just as her mom said, "I can't believe Bert Howington has suddenly become camera shy."

Joyce tried to distract her with the menu. "Have you ever tasted kangaroo, Eleanor?"

"Isn't that the cute critter on your coat of arms?"

Smiling, Joyce said, "Yes, the emu is there too and it's been known to grace our dinner table. I haven't tried it myself, but I'm told it's quite tasty. You know, kangaroo meat is quite lean."

Her mom hummed, "I'm not sure I'd be able eat Skippy."

Joyce looked up. "Oh, here's Abby. I hope you don't mind. We rescued your mom from Markus' clutches. Would you like to join us for dinner?"

"I'm not sure I can fit another meal in just yet," Abby said, "But I'll join you for a while. Although, you look as though you're on a date."

"Nonsense. Sit down."

Abby suspected Joyce had everything under control but it wouldn't hurt to make sure. "Okay. I might nibble on something."

Joyce waited for Abby to settle down and then winked. "Your mom has been telling us about her stroke of good luck. She is so lucky to be getting an original Beatrix Potter illustration."

Abby silently groaned. Why tempt Fate by skating around the subject she most wanted to avoid? Why? Because Joyce obviously couldn't help herself. She enjoyed living dangerously... At someone else's expense.

Using the menu to hide her face, Abby mouthed, "Please change the subject."

Joyce nodded. "Bradford had a new shipment come in today. His uncle had an associate who hunted down estate sales. I think it's marvelous to never have to worry about where his stock is coming from. After all, people die all the time."

She called that changing the subject?

"I love antiques," her mom said. "Joyce, you'll be spoilt for choice when you furnish your new home."

"Yes, Joyce. When are you two getting married?" Abby asked.

"Bradford and I were just talking about that. Life can be so unpredictable. You get up in the morning, and you don't know if you'll make it through to the end of the day. So, we decided to bring the date forward and make the best of the time we're given before either of us kicks the bucket... unexpectedly."

"That's a morbid outlook." Abby looked at Bradford for confirmation but he didn't lift his gaze away from the menu. For all Abby knew, he might have switched off.

Thankfully, the waitress came to take their orders and Joyce turned her focus to what she would have for dinner. However, Abby should have known Joyce wouldn't give up her fun and games.

"I'll have the steak. Rare please. In fact, rare enough for a skilled veterinarian to resurrect it. And for dessert... Let me see. I seem to remember Hannah baking a delightful Death by Chocolate Soufflé. Is that still on the menu?"

"Aren't you concerned about keeping the weight off for your wedding dress?" Abby murmured.

"Oh, I'm having too much fun to worry about that."

Whispering, Abby asked, "Whatever happened to helping me out?"

Joyce winked. "You know me, I like to keep things interesting."

Glancing down at the cell phone, Abby saw her mom looking toward the tourist group table.

"I'd hate to say this, but I'm glad I'm over here instead of with the group," her mom said. "They're not looking as lively as they did yesterday or this morning. I still don't see Bert Howington. Maybe that's why. I should go over and ask about him. He mentioned feeling a little tired early today."

"Really?"

"I wasn't surprised," her mom continued. "He keeps himself engaged in every conversation. And they have been on the trot, every day, for the past two weeks. It takes its toll. Abby, I think the waitress wants to take your order."

"Oh, yes... I'll have some bread and dip, please. Chef's choice."

"Is it just me or is everyone looking a bit mournful?" her mom asked. "Even the music wafting over from the bar is muted."

They all exchanged glances. Abby couldn't tell for sure, but she thought Joyce might have kicked Bradford under the table as a prompt to say something.

Bradford cleared his throat. "It's probably the weather, Eleanor. The forecast is for snow. We haven't had a patch of blue sky in days. Yes, that must be it."

Joyce patted Abby's hand and mouthed, "We've got this."

Thankfully, Joyce gave it a rest and they managed to get through their meal without any mention of the subject Abby wanted to avoid.

"Relax, and have some wine, Abby," Joyce encouraged.

"Thanks, but I already had a beer and I don't like to mix my drinks."

Joyce continued to behave herself by asking Abby's mom about her job as an illustrator but there was only so much talking they could do before her mom found a gap in the conversation.

"I can't believe Bert would leave his group to fend for themselves," her mom said. "I hope he hasn't come down with something."

"Eleanor, you're in for a visual treat," Joyce clapped her hands. "Here comes my Death by Chocolate Soufflé. We're very lucky to have a chef of Hannah's caliber in this little town."

Unfortunately, the soufflé failed to capture her mom's attention which appeared to be fixed on something else.

Her mom sighed. "Abby, I think your detective is trying to catch your attention."

"I don't think so," Abby said. "He went home for the day."

"I'm sure that's him. Look, he's waving."

Abby turned. It was Joshua. "Heavens. Is it that time already? I'd almost forgotten. I... I promised to play a game of darts with him. Excuse me."

Abby rushed toward him, mouthing, "Smile."

His lips moved upward but Abby could tell his heart wasn't in it. This left her in no doubt he had come bearing ill tidings.

"Please tell me this is about you not being able to stay away." Abby tried to smile, but her face tightened. She led him toward the bar. "Am I going to need a drink?"

"Yes."

Abby huffed out a breath. "Okay. Spill."

"According to the pathologist at the hospital, the tablets were beta blockers prescribed to lower blood pressure."

"And?"

"He had a heart condition."

"Are you trying to soften the blow?"

"You should have a drink first," he suggested.

"Now I'm almost afraid to." Abby shook her head. "I think I should keep a clear head."

Joshua nodded and leaned in. "Preliminary tests have raised a few questions, enough to suspect foul play."

"What exactly does that mean?" She knew what it meant but she wanted Joshua to spell it out for her so that she would be left in no doubt whatsoever.

"He found traces of a foreign substance."

Abby tried to let the words sink in and make sense. She tossed them around her mind but she couldn't quite wrap her head around the idea someone had tampered with the medication. "I'll have that drink now, Mitch."

Someone tapped Abby on the shoulder. She turned and found Joyce holding up Abby's cell phone.

"Your mom insisted on speaking with you." Joyce mouthed an apology.

Abby swallowed. "What's up, Mom?"

"Bert Howington might have looked a little tired but he wouldn't leave his friends alone. There's something you're not telling me, Abby. Has something happened to Bert Howington?"

———————

*a*bby made a last-ditch attempt to cover up Bert Howington's death and failed miserably.

"Abby, I can always tell when you're trying to wiggle your way out of telling the truth," her mom warned. "You've been evasive and on edge all day long, and more chatty than usual."

Abby considered opening with something along the lines of… Oh, heavens, she had no idea. Maybe she could remind her mom about Bert feeling tired, and how he might have been trying to play down the warning signs of an impending heart attack.

"Well?" her mom prompted.

"Mom, remember that time you sat me down and told me about the cycle of life."

"Bert Howington is dead?"

Mitch rang the bar bell. Despite his height, he climbed onto a barstool. "Could I have everyone's attention, please. No, this isn't the last call. Folks, the jig is up. Abby gave the game away. You can all relax."

A sigh of relief and a wave of murmurs swept around the bar.

"I see," her mom said. "You were all in on it. What were you thinking, Abby? Were you trying to spare my feelings?"

Abby had to raise her voice to make herself heard above the loud chatter. Mitch's announcement had wound everyone up and they'd launched into an animated discussion of the day's event.

"Abby meant well, Eleanor," Joyce said. "Why don't we go back to our table and we'll fill you in on everything that happened?"

That would only be half the story, Abby thought. She thanked Joyce and, straightening, she finished her drink.

Mitch smiled. "You gave it your best shot, Abby. Here, have a drink on the house."

"Okay, detective. I think we need to take this somewhere else. I can barely hear myself think."

"Yes, that would be a good idea."

Abby waited until they'd reached the safety of her apartment to say, "We need to keep this under wraps. It's bad enough he died. Now you're saying he died under suspicious circumstances. At least, I think that's what you're saying. I'm not sure of anything anymore. It's been a trying day."

Joshua nodded.

"And why are you sharing this information with me?" Abby held her hand up. "Don't get me wrong. I'm grateful to be privy to inside information but the police are not known for breaching protocol."

"Your mom spent some time with the deceased. Has she mentioned anything that might be pertinent? Anything at all."

Abby gave it some thought. "She noticed Bert hadn't been feeling well." Abby tried to remember her mom's exact words. "Not as lively as he'd been. She put it down to being travel weary." Abby got busy lighting the fire. She'd been lucky to land this apartment. The previous occupant had been Mitch's sister, Eddie, and she'd made the place cozy with all the amenities one would enjoy in a normal apartment.

She didn't make any effort to encourage Joshua to say more, taking advantage of the brief respite to get her thoughts into order. But Joshua didn't need encouragement. On the contrary, he appeared to need a sounding board.

"I thought this would be a straightforward death," he said. "The local hospital takes care of doing toxicology screenings but they're simple tests that look for the presence of drugs of abuse in the urine and the blood."

Abby cringed.

"Sorry, is that too much information?" Joshua asked.

"No. Go for it. I need to toughen up."

"It's standard procedure to inform the next of kin of the death first before proceeding from there. If there needs to be an autopsy, the coroner then has to let them know."

Abby nodded. "And, in this case, there will be an autopsy because he died unexpectedly."

"Yes."

Abby knew there were exceptions. If there had been a pre-existing condition with no suspicious circumstances, then there wouldn't be any need for an autopsy. "Did the next of kin have any issues with an autopsy being performed?" it occurred to ask.

"Not exactly. There's a forty-eight hour window of opportunity to lodge an objection and the son wanted the full forty-eight hours to decide. He claimed to be in shock, which is understandable."

"Has that raised suspicions?"

Joshua brushed his hand along the light bristle on his chin. "Not really. In times of grief, people can act out of character. The pathologist ran basic tests and found enough evidence to proceed with an autopsy. That's all we need for now."

"So, Bert Howington didn't die of natural causes." The thought hovered in Abby's mind. She waited a moment to see if it would fade, but it remained in place.

"At least we have a local hospital. Otherwise, the autopsy would have to be performed in Melbourne and that would take time. The evidence is not conclusive, but it's enough to open an investigation."

"Joshua, I still get the feeling you're trying to tell

me something but you don't really want to. Either that, or I'm too jet lagged to follow what you're saying."

He leaned forward, his hands clasped, his head lowered. "The pathologist decided to send the samples to Melbourne for further testing."

Abby's eyes widened. "And he did that because he's suddenly in doubt of his abilities or because he thinks there is something suspicious?" Abby groaned. "I think I'm in denial." In denial. Clinging to hope. Praying this would all go away.

"Sorry." Joshua nodded. "We have a murder on our hands."

Meaning…

They had a killer on the loose.

~

So much for trying to adjust to a different time zone again. Abby looked at her bedside clock. Two in the morning. She had managed to doze off for an hour but had sprung awake with a barrage of thoughts swimming around her mind.

Unable to get back to sleep, she settled on the couch to drink a cup of chamomile tea and trawl through the internet searching for information on heart and blood pressure medicine.

"I hope the police never have reason to look into my search history," she murmured to herself.

Taking a break, she checked her cell phone and read

a message from Faith. "Where did you get to?" In the confusion of her mom finding out about Bert and Joshua telling her about the pathologist's suspicions, she'd forgotten about Faith.

Abby guessed Mitch had filled her in. She sent Faith a text apologizing for missing her the previous night and asking her to organize an extra cell phone, something she knew Faith would enjoy doing.

She couldn't cancel her mom's virtual tour but she needed to stay in touch while doing her best to keep her mom in blissful ignorance of the real facts.

Time to be creative, Abby thought.

Closing her eyes for a moment, Abby tried meditating her way back to sleep. She had a flock of sheep parading around a paddock with an imaginary Doyle doing his best to herd them around. Then Abby remembered she lived in cattle territory, so she mentally replaced the sheep with cattle. Moments later, she felt a wet nose pressing against her cheek.

"Hey, Doyle." Abby stirred and lifted her hand up to her eyes. "Okay. I guess I actually fell asleep. It's morning." And she'd given herself a stiff neck. Sitting up, Abby tried to rub the kink out of her neck. She checked the time. Eight o'clock. Abby cringed and rubbed her neck again. When she tried to straightened, she yelped.

She couldn't straighten.

"Great. I'm going to walk around looking lopsided." All for nothing, she thought since she hadn't come up with any new ideas to manage the out of control situation.

"I'm going to stand under a hot shower. Hopefully, that will fix me."

An hour later, Abby tilted the cell phone and smiled. "Hey, Mom."

"I wondered when you'd connect me. I was just about to call Faith."

"No need. Here we are. Doyle and I, bright-eyed and bushy-tailed." Abby did her best to smile but, going by her mom's expression, she had failed to look convincing.

"Your smile is all crooked. What's wrong, Abby?"

"Nothing."

"I can see the ceiling beam behind you. Everything looks... tilted."

Making her way downstairs, Abby turned the cell phone around and tried to straighten it.

"Now everything is tilting the other way," her mom said. "Abby, what's going on?"

"Maybe it's an earthquake." Abby gave a silent groan.

"All my eye and Betty Martin," her mom said.

Abby laughed as she recalled the game she sometimes played with her mom, each one trying to outdo the other with obscure sayings. "Huh?"

"Now you're trying to distract me," her mom grumbled.

"Honestly, I don't remember." But she knew it had

to be an alternative way of saying nonsense. "You know the rules, I concede. Now you have to tell me."

"Fine. It's a saying from the 1700s used to dismiss someone talking complete nonsense."

"And?"

"And I don't remember the rest... Hang on, it might have been the name of an eccentric Irish theater-owner and actress. Now, tell me what's wrong."

"Nothing but a case of a stiff neck. I slept wrong on the plane and now I'm paying the price." Abby peered inside the dining room and then remembered she no longer had to worry about the coast being clear. "Are you having breakfast too?"

"Yes, and I can't begin to tell you how strange it feels to eat cereal at six in the afternoon on a sweltering day when I'm craving a mimosa." Her mom hummed. "You seem to forget the rules. Now it's your turn to come up with an obscure saying."

Abby sat down by the window and tried to engage her brain. "Ah, Mitch." She filled him in, explaining the game she played with her mom, and asked for suggestions.

"That's cheating," her mom said.

"No, it's not. The rules allow for a helpline."

Mitch handed her the menu. "Here's one. Flemington confetti. That should be a new one for you guys. Flemington is a suburb in Melbourne. It's home to one of Australia's oldest racecourses. That's where the Melbourne Cup is held every year. You know, the race that stops a nation. The saying hails from the 1920s meaning worthless nonsense or gossip and has something to do with the mess of torn up betting slips left at the racecourse after a day's racing."

"Flemington confetti," her mom mused. "I can't wait to use it. I could even tweak it to Kentucky Derby confetti."

"Oh, here comes Markus," Abby said. "Maybe he has one too."

Hearing his name mentioned, Markus' step faltered. He looked about ready to beat a hasty retreat when Mitch pulled him over. "A saying or word for nonsense."

Markus pushed out a breath. His eyebrows drew down as if in thought. "Moonshine on the water."

Abby and her mom were both familiar with it, but not Mitch so Markus explained, "The moon doesn't shine but actually reflects the light of the sun. The saying describes something fake or lacking real substance… Nonsense."

Abby's mom added to that by saying, "I just looked it up. The saying dates back to 1468, so it's probably one of the oldest ones."

Markus grinned. "So, what's all this about?"

"Abby is trying to pull the wool over my eyes," her mom complained. "Again."

"I woke up with a stiff neck. What's wrong with me not wanting you to worry about me?"

Apparently, nothing. Unless Abby became so over-protective she ended up lying.

Mitch handed the order book to Markus and sat down to join her for breakfast.

"Ready to order?" Markus asked.

"Toast, please." Abby needed a break from all the big meals she'd been having or she'd suffer the consequences.

"Could you be more specific?" Markus asked.

"Bread. Sliced and toasted."

"We have some buttery croissants, fresh out of the oven," Markus suggested. "If you really want toast, I'll need you to tell me if you want white bread, whole meal, light rye, dark rye…"

"The croissants sound tempting."

Markus grinned and strode off. "Coming right up."

"Looks like you're not getting any breakfast," Abby whispered.

Mitch sighed. "Oh, I will get breakfast but it'll be up to Markus to decide what he brings me." Mitch nudged her under the table with his foot and signaled with his eyes.

Abby turned toward the window and saw Faith striding toward the Gazette, her attention on the cell phone in her hand. Abby knew the precise moment Faith read the message she'd sent in the early hours of the morning. Faith swung on her feet and headed in the opposite direction, presumably to purchase another cell phone.

Half an hour later, Mitch received a text. He looked up and smiled. "If you had to buy a new phone, would you care about the brand?"

Abby shook her head. "Not particularly. Why do you ask?"

Mitch bobbed his eyebrows up and down.

Oh… Right. Faith had found a way to communicate with her through Mitch. "I think I'd be happy with anything I don't have to spend too much time learning how to use."

"In other words, keep it simple," Mitch said as he keyed in a text message forwarding the instructions to Faith.

Sitting back, Abby sipped her coffee. For a moment, she forgot about the last twenty-four hours and enjoyed the peaceful silence.

The Gloriana's coffee had never been as good as Joyce's. Made from the same beans, the Faydon brothers just hadn't quite been able to pull it off. Abby knew they'd switched off when Joyce had shown them how to brew the perfect cup. At one point, Abby had suspected Joyce of leaving out a key step in the process, but she knew better now. "Is Frankie not working today?" The latest addition to Eden had recently started working at the pub. Her vast experience had included working as a barista and her skills were beyond compare. Even Joyce had been impressed.

"She's taking a couple of days off. Why do you ask?" Mitch grinned. "Is the coffee not up to scratch?"

"I guess she hasn't had time to train you."

"This is disturbing," her mom said.

Abby glanced down at her cup of coffee. It remained half full. Two more minutes and she would have finished it. Now it wouldn't taste the same.

"What is?" she asked.

"While you were having breakfast, I decided to check my email. There's one from Bert's daughter. It's an order to cease and desist."

Abby straightened. "Tommy-rot."

"It looks official," her mom said.

"Not if it's an email. I'm sure an official cease and desist document has to come from a lawyer." Abby leaned down and tried to read the printout her mom held up.

Mitch cleared his throat. "Can you back up a bit and explain Tommy-rot."

Without taking her eyes off the cell phone, Abby said, "Tommy was a nickname for the poor-quality bread doled out to soldiers in the 18th century. In the Victorian era, it eventually came to mean nonsense." Abby finished scanning the page and growled. "How did his daughter get Bert's email?"

"What does it say?" Mitch asked.

"Bert Howington's daughter is asking my mom to stop pestering him for that Beatrix Potter illustration he promised to give her." According to her mom, Bert had sent the email the previous morning. That had been quick work on the daughter's part. "How did she gain access to his emails so quickly?" And how could she take such prompt action? She'd only recently heard about her dad's heart attack. "This is so wrong, on so many levels."

"Yeah, Tommy-rot," Mitch said.

"Disregard it, Mom. Bert's email to you can count as a last wish. He wanted you to have the drawing."

"I won't push for it," her mom said. "This must be her way of dealing with her loss."

"Doesn't it strike you as cold-blooded and calculating?" If Abby lost her mom, she would be catatonic. She picked up her cup of coffee but couldn't bring herself to drink it. Bound to leave a bad taste in her mouth, Abby thought.

Sitting back, she looked out the window and thought about Sebastian Cavendish, the current owner of the Eden Rise Gazette. She'd met him when she'd first arrived in Eden, but she hadn't seen him since. It didn't surprise Abby. The man had bigger fish to fry. As the owner of a national daily newspaper and stakeholder in other international businesses, he spent little time in the country. If anyone had a way of getting their hands on an original Beatrix Potter illustration, he would. She'd seen her mom's eyes brighten at the prospect of owning one. If she wanted one, she would have one…

"Mom, don't worry about it. In fact, don't even answer the email. If she gets in touch with you again, let me know. I'm sure there are other Beatrix Potter illustrations floating around the place."

"Abby, that's the least of my concerns. I'm not entirely comfortable being labeled a gold-digger."

Abby leaned forward. "She actually said that?"

"In the postscript."

Abby had a good mind to sue the woman for defamation. Gold-digger, indeed. Bert Howington had wanted to give away the illustration. It had been his to give.

"Here comes Faith," Mitch murmured.

Faith strode in, all smiles and cheerful greetings for a not so sunny morning. She waited until she knew Abby's mom couldn't see her to wave the new cell phone Abby had asked for.

Sitting down opposite Abby, she scrawled the new number on a piece of paper and added a brief note.

Good to go, Abby read.

"Where is everyone?" Faith asked. "Usually, the dining room is buzzing at this time of morning."

Hearing a commotion coming from the bar, Abby turned.

A woman burst into the dining room. "Where is she?"

Markus appeared behind her and warned, "This is a hostile free environment. If you don't behave, I'll have to ask you to vacate the premises."

"Yeah, you and whose army?" the woman asked.

Mitch surged to his feet and strode up to her, his stride easy and, Abby imagined, his smile in place. "Is there a problem here?"

"She's Mr. Howington's daughter," Markus said. "She's demanding to get access to his room, but the police called a few minutes ago and asked me to keep it locked. Now she's after a gold-digger. I told her we don't have any of those around."

"I know she's here," the woman roared. "And she's not the only one."

Chapter Six

"The woman must have hit the road at the crack of dawn to get here so early." None of the tourists staying at the pub had made an appearance downstairs. Abby could only assume they too had received threatening emails from Mr. Howington's daughter.

After accusing Abby's mom of being a gold-digger, Denise Lowe had gone on a rampage, demanding to be allowed access to her dad's room. Luckily the police had shown up and had taken control of the situation.

"I'm trying to make allowances for her grief," Faith said, "But the woman is scary."

"Let's hope she gets everything sorted out today," Abby mused. "I wouldn't want her staying at the pub. Doyle appears to be taking a day off, so I'd have to look over my shoulder…"

"Are we setting up our office at the pub?" Faith asked.

Abby gave a small distracted nod. "It's where the action seems to be." She knew Faith had the office phone diverted to her cell phone so if any calls came in they would go straight to her. Right on cue, her cell rang.

"Eden Rise Gazette," Faith chirped. "Ah, detective. Top of the morning to you. You're on your way to the pub? I see. Oh… Oh, my. Well, let me tell you, there's been quite a commotion here this morning. Our star reporter is on the scene. Yes, I'll pass on the message."

"Let me guess." Abby bobbed her head from side to side and winced. Knowing Joshua, he would have further instructions for her, drawing lines in the sand and whatnot. "He wants me to hold back on printing a story."

Faith leaned forward and checked Abby's cell. Her mom had taken a break to have a coffee with her neighbor so they were in the clear.

"Joshua wanted to know if you'd had a chance to speak with your mom."

"He must be stepping up the investigation." Her mom had spent an entire morning with the tourist group. Maybe she had overheard something. She'd definitely had her eyes peeled, noticing people's odd behavior. If Abby asked the right questions, her mom might remember noticing something else. But she'd have to be careful how she phrased her questions.

The jig was by no means up, Abby thought. If this turned out to be a murder, her mom would never come to visit.

Mitch brought them each a fresh cup of coffee and pulled up a chair. "Any news?"

Abby looked over her shoulder and toward the bar. "The police managed to corral Denise Lowe at the other end of the bar. A police officer is standing guard outside Bert Howington's room, or so Markus tells me. I haven't been upstairs yet. I assume Joshua is going to have another look through the room." She also assumed he had more news from the pathologist. She closed her eyes and sipped her coffee. "You might as well know, Joshua has opened up an investigation."

Faith and Mitch stared at her.

Abby didn't want to jump the gun. After all, the pathologist needed to receive the final report. Until then, they couldn't be sure Bert's medication had been tampered with but, if it had been, that would be the obvious cause of death. As for motive... Well, the man had won a great deal of money. That made him an easy and obvious target. "There appear to be suspicious circumstances." Bert had looked fit and healthy. Sure, he'd had a heart condition, but she assumed he'd had it under control.

His daughter would definitely have more information. If she had access to his email account, she would also, most likely... hopefully, have known about his medication and treatment.

"Is that why you were asking about the tourists who'd been downstairs last night?" Mitch asked.

Abby sighed and looked heavenward. She didn't want to be the type of person who always expected the worst. She'd asked Mitch about the tourists even before Joshua had told her about the pathologist's concerns. "I can't remember what I'd been thinking at the time."

"Your reporter's natural curiosity at work," Faith said. "You must have sensed something in the air."

Flicking through the photos on her cell phone, Abby selected one and forwarded it to Faith. "I just sent you a photo. The morning mom joined the tourist group, she asked me to take a photo of them and everyone has name tags on." Which would make identifying them easy.

"Are we setting up a crime board?" Faith asked.

"We might have to," Abby mused and brushed her fingers across her forehead. Had the seed of suspicion lodged in her mind even before Joshua had mentioned anything about the pathologist's concerns?

The night before Bert Howington had died, her mom had asked her to hold the cell phone up so she could wave goodnight. Abby hoped she'd be able to remember if anyone had been missing from the group. With Joshua investigating, she figured he'd need all the help he could get. One never knew what sort of information might help pinpoint a suspect.

Faith surged to her feet. "I'll go back to the office and get the photo printed out."

Abby gulped down her coffee. "Can you do me a favor, Mitch? I'm going upstairs. If my mom comes back, can you keep her entertained?"

He grinned. "I'm happy to help. It's been a quiet morning."

On her way upstairs, Abby came across Doyle curled up by the fireplace. He appeared to be content, so she left him to enjoy his nap.

Upstairs, she encountered a police officer standing outside Bert Howington's room. As she reached her apartment, Markus came around the corner.

"Markus!"

He took in her smile and frowned. "That's the look of a woman who wants something."

"A tiny favor. Do you have any vacant rooms?"

"There's one."

"Is it ready for the next guest?" she asked.

"The rooms are always kept ready."

She held up a finger. "One more question. Do all the rooms have the same setup?"

He shrugged. "Basic furniture. Tea and coffee making facilities. The usual."

Abby clicked her fingers and tried to put her thoughts into order. "Will it be possible for me to have a look inside the room?"

Markus leaned in and smiled. "Only if you tell me why."

"I'm not sure yet." She'd only had a glimpse inside Bert's room when Joshua had gone in to search for the medicine, but the mind tended to absorb more information than one could feasibly remember actually seeing.

"When you figure it out will you tell me then?" Markus asked.

Abby grinned. "Of course."

He drew out a key and signaled for her to follow him. As they walked past the police officer, Markus nodded and offered him a cup of coffee.

Unlocking the door, he pushed it open and waved her in. "Talk me through it."

The room looked exactly like Bert Howington's room. Abby swept her gaze over all the surfaces and tried to memorize where everything sat. The kettle. The coffee canister. The selection of tea bags and a couple of mugs.

She peered inside a small basket. "What's this?"

"It's our complimentary basket with a few essentials." He shrugged. "Hand lotion. Face moisturizer. Things guests might forget to bring with them. We might be a small-town pub but we like to provide extra perks."

She switched her attention to everything that looked different. The bed had been made with military precision. She could see the cleanliness but she could also smell it. Bert's bed hadn't been made and while the room had looked and smelled clean, Abby remembered noticing a lived-in look about it.

"Now, are you going to share?" Markus asked.

Abby smiled. "My mom and I used to play a game.

She would set a few objects on a table and ask me to look at them, then she would cover them with a cloth and remove one of the items without me seeing it. After a few minutes, she would remove the cloth and ask me to identify the missing item."

Markus grinned. "I used to play that game too. It's a memory game. I'd set a plate of food in front of Mitch, ask him to cover his eyes. Then I'd wolf it all down and ask him where it had disappeared to."

"Yeah, something like that. So, when I have a look inside Bert's room, I can compare it to this one. I'm hoping to pick up on something that maybe shouldn't be there, or something missing."

"You're assuming Joshua will give you access to the room. There's a police officer standing outside now, but I'm guessing he'll put some crime scene tape up. That is, assuming a crime has been committed."

Huffing out a breath, Abby said, "Well, I can cash in my chips. Joshua owes me. By his own admission, I've been an asset and quite helpful." Of course, if push came to shove, she'd find a way to access the room.

~

"What do you mean I can't go in?" Abby's fingers curled into the palm of her hands. "You know I can help."

"It's not my call, Abby." Giving her an apologetic smile, Joshua strode off.

"Hey, I need to get to my apartment," Abby called out.

Joshua raised his hand and waved it. "Sorry. It'll have to wait."

Pending an investigation. Standing at the end of the hallway, Abby tried to see past the broad-shouldered police officer, but he took a step forward and blocked her entire view.

Abby grumbled. Swinging around, she stomped down the stairs. Okay, so the police had to do their job, but she could help.

Seeing her, Markus leaned against the counter and asked, "Well?"

"I have been arbitrarily dismissed." Abby slumped down on a barstool.

Markus grumbled.

"My thoughts exactly."

"It's that city detective," Markus said. "I knew he'd be trouble when he waltzed into the bar and everyone took a step back, as if he were Moses parting the waves."

"Why did he come? We have a perfectly good police force here."

"I think the family insisted." Markus shifted. "So, what now? You know we'll help in any way we can."

"Thank you, Markus. I think we should wait and see what happens. Joshua is bound to come to his senses and let me take a peek inside the room."

Markus drummed his fingers on the counter. "There's

always a way. If they leave the police officer standing guard outside the room, you can use the fire escape ladder to access the room. I'm sure you'll exercise due diligence and not meddle with possible evidence."

Abby's eyebrows rose. "Ladder?"

Markus nodded. "We're only required to have two emergency exits but a couple of years ago we decided to take extra steps and install ladders outside each window."

Abby decided now wouldn't be a good time to tell Markus about her fear of heights. She couldn't even stand on a chair without feeling wobbly.

"What about the window?" Abby asked. "It's bound to be locked."

Markus grinned. "No, it's not. When a room is unoc-cupied, we leave the window partly open to air out the room. In Bert's case, the maid left the window open because that's the way he liked it. I believe it's still open."

"Okay." Finally, something working in her favor.

"What time should we rendezvous?" Markus asked, his eyes sparkling with enthusiasm.

"Huh?"

"I'm thinking we should do it in the dead of night. Sometime around two in the morning." He brushed his hand across his chin. "No, scratch that. We should do it when the pub is at its busiest. That way, if you make a noise, the police won't hear you."

Abby lowered her gaze and gave the idea some thought. Did she want to tread on Joshua's toes? What if she got him into trouble? "How about we use it as a backup plan? In case Joshua doesn't change his mind."

Markus looked at her, eyes unblinking. "You don't like the idea."

"Oh... No, I think it's a splendid plan. And, thank you for suggesting it, but the police have a job to do and I really don't want to make any waves." She returned to the dining room where she'd spent most of the morning and found Faith typing away on her laptop. "What are you working on?"

"The layout for this week's newspaper." Faith held her gaze for a moment and then smiled. "Okay, that's not exactly true. I'm only trying to look busy."

"That works for me."

"Mitch is the only one run off his feet," Faith said. "The tourists have been asking for room service all morning."

Right on cue, Mitch whizzed by saying, "I'll be with you shortly."

"I guess Hannah is busy too. She's baking up a storm." Faith looked at some notes. "Your mom is taking a nap and said to tell you she's having dinner with one of her neighbors." Faith reached inside her bag. "If you need a distraction, you could take a look at these. I took the liberty of reading them."

"And?"

Faith gave her a small smile. "They're all anonymous and they're all asking for advice."

"Huh? Advice? From me?"

"Yes. In fact, they're all addressed to Dear Abby."

"But we're not running an advice column."

"But we could. In fact, there's nothing stopping us. You already have a handful of letters. If you write a column, that will encourage other people to write in. If you build it, they will come."

Abby scanned through one of the letters. "This person is asking advice about lamingtons. I don't know the first thing about them."

"Yes, you do. They're yummy and they're covered in chocolate."

"Hang on. Isn't there some sort of controversy about them?"

"Oh, yes. The Lamington Wars."

"Do I want to become involved in them?"

Faith shrugged. "Why not? It would be fun. You're still relatively new in town, so you can play that card. You know, the innocent card. And you could remain impartial. Like a referee."

"I don't know." She set the letter down. "I'll think about it."

Straightening, Faith signaled with her eyes and just to make sure she had Abby's attention, she nudged her with her foot. "The city detective is leaving."

Abby swung around and saw Joshua walking out with the detective. She didn't see the police officer leave, so she guessed that meant he'd been posted outside the room until further notice.

Where's the trust? Abby thought. "I'm going to take Doyle for a walk. If any of the tourists come down, let me know. I won't go far."

"Hang on. I just received a text from Joshua. He's coming back and wants to talk with you. I'm sending him your new number so he can text you directly."

Five minutes later Joshua strode in, his mouth set into a grim line. "Sorry about earlier."

Abby prayed he hadn't been put on a tight leash. It would make her work that much harder. "I need to go upstairs to my apartment. Am I allowed to?"

"Of course, but don't ask me to let you inside Bert Howington's room."

"I guess that means you've now launched a full-scale investigation."

Nodding, he raked his fingers through his hair.

"You're not at liberty to say?"

A group of people walked into the bar. With lunch about to get on its way, she realized she'd been at the pub all morning waiting for something to happen. She suddenly understood why the people of Eden made their own entertainment.

"Denise Lowe has some connections high up," he said. "On the one hand, we have to deal with a city detective, but on the other hand, he's not giving her any preferential treatment so the room is still out of bounds to her."

SONIA PARIN

"Apart from the medication you took, did you remove anything else from the room?" Abby asked. When he shook his head, she asked, "Is there anything new you can tell me or maybe confirm something?"

He nodded. "I can confirm that Bert Howington had been taking beta blockers to slow his heart rate."

Frowning, Abby said, "I thought you said the medication was for his blood pressure."

"Apparently the blood pressure is lowered by slowing the heart rate. It has something to do with blocking the adrenaline that gets the heart pumping hard. Anyhow, tests have identified a foreign substance in his body."

"Yes, you've already mentioned that. Do you want me to guess what it is?"

"Sorry, I'm still processing the last few hours." He waved his hand. "The preliminary tests show significant traces of digitalis."

"I'm confused. Isn't that used for heart treatments?" Abby asked.

Joshua shrugged.

"But the digitalis was in his system," Abby said, running the fact through her mind. "I'm guessing the significant amounts were enough to affect the medicine he'd been taking."

"Yes. It produces a slowing of the heart rate which, if maintained, usually produces a massive heart attack."

And Bert Howington had already been taking

medication to slow his heart-rate... "How did he ingest the digitalis and why?"

"That's what we don't know. His daughter couldn't shed any light on the matter. People with health issues sometimes seek alternative forms of treatment without consulting their doctors, but that doesn't appear to be the case here. She'd been very close to her dad. In fact, despite being married and running her own household, she used to visit him every morning. She hired staff to do the cleaning and cooking and she maintained the household accounts. Basically, she ran his life."

"How do you know she'd share information with you?"

The remark appeared to catch Joshua by surprise.

"Just saying. If she wanted her dad dead, she would have had the opportunity to meddle. She definitely had the motive."

Joshua looked surprised.

"Oh, come on. I thought the police always suspected the closest relatives first." Abby tilted her head in thought. "This city detective has you all worked up."

"I guess I don't work well with the suffer-no-fools type. He's old school and doesn't give an inch."

Abby smiled. "So, we're still friends?"

"That depends. Can you keep a low profile?"

Abby read between the lines. She could snoop around so long as she didn't involve him directly. "Sure, I can go undercover."

"How about taking a back seat on this one?" he asked.

"You know that's asking too much. I'll try but I can't promise anything. Denise Lowe accused my mom of being a gold-digger. That doesn't sit well with me."

～

Abby hunted down Doyle's tartan winter jacket. After several hours of sitting around waiting for something to happen, she had finally decided to take Doyle for a much-needed walk. Before she strode out of her apartment, she looked out the window.

Taking a deep breath, she looked down.

The ground seemed to be a long way down.

Taking another deep breath, she opened the window and peered out. Holding on tight to the window sill, she leaned out further and managed to see the fire escape ladder attached to the outside wall.

Gritting her back teeth, she leaned out even further. Sure enough, there were ladders all along the wall next to all the windows.

She could do this. Yes, she could…

Downstairs, she found Doyle still curled up by the fireplace. The moment he saw her, he put his little paw over his eye.

"I know you're awake."

He huffed out a breath and gave her a wag of his tail.

"Come on. Time to stretch our legs. You'll have to wear this. Don't grumble. It's tartan. It's very manly. Millions of Scotsmen wear it."

In the time she'd been upstairs, the pub had filled up with customers coming in for lunch. The topic of conversation remained focused on Bert's sudden death. No one had ever died outside The Gloriana, at least, not within the last one hundred years. This launched a debate about what other types of deaths might be included because, apparently, over a hundred years before there had been an incident involving a horse drawn carriage and a man who'd been celebrating striking gold.

Outside, she rounded the corner and came across Mitch helping to unload boxes from a truck. "Is this the delivery entrance?" Abby asked and looked down the alleyway.

Mitch nodded. "The kitchen delivery entrance is down the end."

And the alleyway was kept secure with a large six-foot steel gate. "Is this gate kept locked all the time?"

"Sure is."

"What about in case of an emergency?"

"It can be unlocked from the inside."

"So, anyone needing to use the fire escape ladder would be able to make a quick getaway," Abby mused.

"Are you planning on skipping town without paying your bill?"

No, Abby thought, she wanted to plot out her break-in. Her legs quivered. The first floor looked to be a long way up. She assumed Mitch would lock the gate when he finished. She also assumed Markus would open it up for her.

She followed Mitch along the alleyway. Looking up, she asked, "Where's my window?"

"The corner."

"Oh." She counted the next two windows and went to stand directly below what had been Bert Howington's room.

Mitch came to stand beside her. "What are we looking at?"

Abby held a finger up, "Hang on." She answered her cell on the second ring. "Faith."

"Your mom wants to connect with you," Faith said.

Abby retrieved her other cell phone. Both Doyle and Mitch looked at her. As she answered, she reached for the bottom of the ladder and pulled it down.

"Oh, you're out and about," her mom said.

Abby kept the cell phone pointed at herself. "Hi, Mom. How was your lunch or was it your dinner?" As she listened, she set her foot on the first rung. The distraction worked a treat. Usually, her thighs quivered with anxiety at the prospect of scaling any heights. She felt a twinge, but nothing to really worry about.

"Mitch, what's Abby up to?" her mom demanded.

"Mom! You can't put Mitch on the spot."

"I'd only be putting him on the spot if he had to lie on your behalf."

Mitch grinned. "Abby's taking Doyle for a walk, Eleanor."

Her mom harrumphed. "This looks like an alley."

Mitch switched on his charm. "That's because it is. When I saw Abby, I stopped her for a chat, as one does."

"I see," her mom said. "Abby has enlisted you as a co-conspirator."

Chapter Seven

"The tourists must have all gone out the residents' door. I didn't see them leave but they're all at Joyce's Café," Abby said as she pushed the door open. "Would you like to catch up with them, Mom?" Abby knew she was tempting fate as any one of them could mention something about the police being at the pub, something that would trigger a barrage of questions Abby wouldn't know how to answer.

"No, that's fine. I'd like to spend more time with you, dear."

And find out what she'd been up to with Mitch, Abby thought. Well, she had some digging of her own to do. Abby headed straight to a table by the window and sat down to study the menu. Doyle, enjoying the special privilege of being the only dog in town allowed inside the café, made the rounds of the tables to soak up some attention.

Abby adjusted the cell phone so her mom could see the table with the tourists.

"I wonder if any of them received cease and desist emails?" Abby asked as she continued to peruse the menu.

"I'm sure Alice did too," her mom murmured.

"Oh?"

"I caught the tail end of a couple of conversations. She mentioned being strapped for cash and I saw Bert putting his hand over hers as if to reassure her. I think he might have bailed her out."

Wow. She'd read all that from a simple gesture?

"I also heard her say he was a lifesaver. I think it's safe to assume Bert offered to help her out."

"Did she ever say where she knew him from?" Abby asked.

"From way back. I heard her make a couple of reminiscing remarks. You know the type. Do you remember when the four of us... So, I assume she was referring to her husband and Bert's wife."

Would Alice bite the hand that fed her? Assuming Bert had offered financial assistance, Alice would not have wanted anything to happen to him.

If not money, what other motive could there be for murder? Jealousy? "You mentioned someone else had been vying for his attention."

Her mom chuckled. "They all were. Including me. I enjoyed his conversations. I couldn't help thinking Bert would be a lovely companion sitting by the fireplace on a cold winter night, chatting and..." her mom sighed. "I've heard some young people complain how difficult it is to meet someone nice. They have no idea what it's like when you get older."

Abby had never heard her mom complain of loneliness. What if she had mentioned something and Abby had missed it?

"It's silly," her mom said. "I didn't think I'd ever feel this way again."

Abby saw her chance to encourage her mom and took it. "Just think how many more people you'd meet if you traveled."

"Yes, I have been playing around with the idea."

Abby crossed her fingers and took this as a good sign. "Are there any wallflowers in the group?" she asked before her mom overanalyzed the idea of traveling. Someone sitting back, listening, watching, waiting... would be an ideal suspect.

"There is one woman." Abby heard her mom click her fingers. "I'll have to think about her name. Isn't that dreadful. She mostly sat back and listened."

Abby peered over at the table where the tourists had settled and tried to pick out the wallflower. It wasn't as easy as she'd thought since everyone appeared to be in a somber mood.

"Is it the woman in the pink sweater?" Abby asked.

"Yes. What made you think she's the wallflower?"

"She's the only one sitting back. The others are all leaning forward. They appear to engage more easily."

"Yes, I tried speaking with her but she mostly smiled and nodded. She went to school with Bert and became an accountant too."

Had she followed that career path because she'd wanted to follow in the footsteps of her dream man?

"Did Bert pay much attention to her?" Abby asked.

"Bert gave everyone the same amount of attention," her mom offered. "In fact, he made sure to include everyone in the conversations." Her mom clicked her fingers again. "Cynthia. That's her name."

Had Cynthia misunderstood Bert's attention? Had she come to the realization he hadn't meant anything by it? Had that driven her to commit a crime of passion, thinking that if she couldn't have him, then no one else would?

"Ready to order?" Joyce asked as she approached their table. Seeing Abby looking at the tourists, she drew out a chair and sat down. "Let me guess, you're here to spy on my customers."

"If I were, I would have sat closer to them." Abby grinned. "Have you heard anything useful?"

"They've been discussing their travel plans and wondering if they should continue with the trip." Joyce leaned in and whispered, "I heard one say the bus company won't issue a refund and that Bert would have wanted them to go on. What do you make of that?"

Bert had picked up the tab for the trip. Had Denise Lowe pulled the plug and demanded a refund?

Joyce gave a knowing smile. "You're thinking the daughter has put a stop to the sponging."

"How do you know about her?" Joyce hadn't been anywhere near the pub when Denise Lowe had shown up.

"Never underestimate the power of the Eden grapevine." Joyce sat back and smiled. "It's giving the Eden Rise Gazette a run for its money."

Her mom cleared her throat. "Abby, take me over to the tourist table. I'd like to find out if any of them received cease and desist emails."

～

"That woman is asking for trouble," her mom mused. "She's tried to get a refund for the tour bus and is threatening to sue them right along with Bert's friends for abusing his generosity."

Despite Abby's concerns, the tourists had been too self-absorbed to mention anything about the police being at the pub.

"Denise Lowe must have money to splurge around on legal fees," Abby said.

"Well, if she didn't before, she certainly does now," her mom remarked. "She's a beneficiary in the will. Bert confided in Alice. Oh, and he wasn't just an accountant. He owned a firm. She'll be getting millions. Whatever Bert spent on this trip is nothing but a drop in the ocean, but she clearly wants every last penny."

Great, Abby groaned. The tourists had the perfect motive to kill Denise Lowe but they weren't investigating her death. Hearing her other cell phone beep, Abby coughed.

"Are you coming down with something?" her mom asked when Abby continued coughing.

"Dust motes," Abby said. Unfortunately, she said it within Joyce's hearing.

"Dust motes?" Joyce exclaimed. "Are you suggesting my café is dusty? For your information, I have an air purifier installed."

"My apologies." Abby lowered her head in a show of humble submission and smiled. "I guess I nearly choked on a crumb." That only made it worse as Joyce launched into a diatribe about the health hazard of not swallowing properly. However, it worked in Abby's favor as her mom turned her attention to Joyce, leaving Abby free to read the text message from Joshua and reply to it.

Denise Lowe had challenged the will because Bert had left a considerable amount of money to all his friends, Abby read. She'd sent everyone an email warning them to not get too cozy with the idea of getting something.

Abby sent Joshua a text asking if he could think of any way to find out if any of Bert's friends knew beforehand they'd be receiving money from Bert. If he'd spoken about leaving money to his daughter, then he might have mentioned spreading the joy and leaving money to them too, Abby thought. She followed that message with another one telling him to find out if any of them had been experiencing financial difficulties. She also told him about Alice being strapped for cash.

"I hadn't realized Joyce could be so sensitive," her mom said.

"It's all part of the entertainment, Mom. I wouldn't take her too seriously." Abby sat back and stared into space. "Mom? What's the first thing you'd do if you knew you were about to receive a large sum of money?"

"I would probably hire a bodyguard to accompany me on a trip to visit you."

"What about the average person? What do you think they'd do?"

"Go on a spending spree. Especially if they'd been experiencing financial difficulties. Of course, there would always be an exception. If they'd been experiencing real financial woes and suddenly received a windfall, they might be sensible and engage a financial advisor."

Abby sent Joshua another text telling him he might want to follow up on that. Maybe someone had already set the ball rolling. While the tourists had spent most of the day in their rooms, they all had access to the Internet...

"Anything else?" Joshua texted back.

Not one to miss an opportunity, Abby sent him another text saying she'd let him know if she thought of anything else.

~

"The perpetrator wore head to toe black," Abby said under her breath as she trudged her way along the dark alleyway, making sure to stay as close to the wall as she could to avoid being seen by anyone looking out their windows.

Earlier, Abby had offered to drive her mom around so she could take in more of the sights, but her mom had wanted to return to the pub where she could keep a close eye on Denise Lowe who hadn't moved away from a corner table. Their return to the pub could not have been timed better. The aroma of Hannah's baking had been impossible to resist so Abby had indulged in some freshly baked pastries rich with crème patisserie and quince paste.

Bert's daughter remained in Eden, biding her time at the pub. According to Mitch, she'd demanded a room at the pub but Mitch had been unable... unwilling to accommodate her. Abby's relief at hearing this had been short-lived as Mitch had told her Denise had managed to book a room at the local bed & breakfast.

"She's tempting fate," Abby murmured under her breath. Contesting the will would make a lot of people unhappy. Of course, she was well within her rights, but it seemed petty.

Joshua had been forthcoming with some information about Denise. She lived in one of Melbourne's most affluent suburbs, her husband headed a large corporation and she wanted for nothing. Except for more of what she already had, Abby thought as she looked up at the first-floor window.

Abby had hoped Markus would be here to hold the ladder for her but he'd assured her the ladder had been bolted against the wall and she would be safe. Besides, the pub had come alive with customers and he had work to do.

"I believe he bailed out at the last minute. So, it's just you and me, Doyle. Remember, you're here to keep watch. If anyone approaches, bark once." She smiled to herself as she suddenly pictured Doyle running for his life and leaving her to face the music.

She took a moment to adjust her belt. "Yes, I admit, this is taking precautions to the extreme." When she'd told Mitch about her plans, she'd been honest enough to come clean about her fear of heights. After having a good laugh at her expense, he'd suggested using his rock-climbing gear, promising to secure some hooks along each rung for her. She only needed to hitch herself to them as she made her way up. When Mitch had offered her a helmet she had thought it would be too much. However, she'd decided to err on the side of caution. One dizzy spell, one slip of the hand... Yeah, she'd wear the helmet.

Adjusting it, she took a closer look at the ladder and growled. "Are you kidding me?"

Mitch had been having a laugh at her expense. She

knew enough about rock-climbing to understand there needed to be a rope…

"Fine. No rope and no hooks equal no climbing." Yes, but… What if she found new information that could prove useful to Joshua's investigation?

Abby brushed her sweaty palms against her jeans. She'd have to do this the old-fashioned way, one rung at a time. Gripping a small flashlight between her teeth, she filled her mind with as many thoughts as she could fit in there, including a few nursery rhymes. The distraction worked until she got half way up. Her hands felt clammy. She huffed out several breaths. Her heart pumped hard against her chest. She could do this, so long as she plastered herself against the ladder and held on for dear life.

Heaving herself up another rung, she took a moment to ease her breath out. "Remind me again why I'm doing this?" she asked herself.

"Come on. You're nearly there."

"Huh?" Abby looked up and saw Markus leaning out of the window. "What… What are you doing there?"

Markus grinned. "The police officer went home."

Abby's mouth gaped open. She felt a scream scramble up to her throat.

"Hey, Abby," Mitch called out from the ground. "Markus sent me to tell you the police officer went home. The coast is clear. You can go in through the door."

Abby made the mistake of looking down.

"Don't look down," Markus warned.

A bead of perspiration trickled down her forehead, slid along her nose and hung there for a second before falling. Gritting her back teeth, Abby reached up and grabbed hold of the next rung but then she felt a big hand taking hold of her and hauling her up the rest of the way.

"Hello," Markus gave a throaty chuckle and tapped her helmet. "You did well, young grasshopper."

She could hear Mitch laughing and knew she'd been well and truly had. "This is about you making your own entertainment," Abby accused as Markus pulled her through the open window. "Admit it."

"Do you blame us? Look at you! You're a regular rock-climbing cat burglar. We're going to be talking about this for days."

"You know I could have been seriously injured."

"You need to embrace the Zen. You're here now. Safe and sound."

"No thanks to you." Abby looked around the room and took a moment to catch her breath. "Has Joshua given Denise Lowe access to the room?"

Markus shrugged. "I've no idea. If he contacted her, I'm sure she would have rushed here straightaway."

Grumbling, Abby wiped her hand along her forehead and got to work. Despite the police doing a thorough search, the room looked the same way it had looked when Joshua had come in to get Bert's heart medication.

Abby drew out her cell phone. After taking photos of the entire room and everything in it she called Joshua. He answered on the second ring. "Did you guys test the water in the jug?"

"Yes."

She opened the coffee canister and sniffed it. "What about the coffee?"

"Why are you asking?"

"I'm sitting here at the pub, drumming my fingers. Humor me."

"Yes to the coffee too."

"And his medication hasn't been tampered with?"

"No."

Somehow, Bert Howington had ingested lethal amounts of digitalis. But how? He'd appeared to have been a happy person, eager to enjoy himself and share his winnings with friends. Could he have sabotaged his own medication? "Were the amounts of foxglove... digitalis found in his system consistent with the amounts required for an overdose... or to significantly slow his heart rate?"

"We're still waiting for the full lab report but..."

"Joshua. Please spare me the official police statement."

Joshua's breath came out in a weary huff. "As I told you, the amounts were disconcerting enough for the pathologist to send samples to Melbourne for further testing. So, I guess my answer is a tentative yes. The digitalis is a contributing factor in his death."

"So, we're looking for traces of digitalis," Abby murmured under her breath. She dug her fingers through her hair and tried to imagine how she would go about introducing the substance into... His food? Just about anything could be reduced to powder form. Maybe someone had carried it around and spiked Bert's food or drinks. If it could be inhaled, the powder might have been sprinkled on his pillow. "I think I saw someone in his room but I can't be sure."

Joshua's tone hardened. "You wait until now to tell me?"

"As I said, I can't be sure what I saw. I'd had a couple of beers..."

"Three," Markus said.

Abby bobbed her head from side to side. "Okay, I had three beers. What with the long flight and long drive, I'm surprised I even made it up the stairs. The person opened and closed the door so quickly, I didn't get a proper look."

Mitch strode in with Doyle.

"Okay," Joshua said. "I'm going to ask Markus to let you inside Bert Howington's room."

Abby gave a nervous chuckle. "Oh... Great."

Markus' cell phone rang. Clearly, Joshua had wasted no time contacting him. "Are you sure you want me to let the snoopy reporter in?" Markus grinned at her.

In the next instant, Joshua appeared at the door, a cell phone in each hand. "You're not the only one with two cell phones."

Doyle barked and scurried to stand in front of Abby. "Oh, yes. Now you bark."

Mitch and Markus excused themselves and left Abby to face the music. Cowards, Abby thought.

"You are relentless." Joshua barely managed to contain his laughter.

Abby grinned. "And thank goodness for that?"

He scanned the room. "Did you touch anything?"

"Heavens, no. What if I left a fingerprint? I wouldn't want to incriminate myself. Being held under suspicion once has been enough." She pointed at a coffee cup. "Has it been tested for residue?"

Joshua nodded. "Swabbed."

Abby picked up a teabag from a basket which held a selection of different flavors. "This is a needle in a haystack. You'd have to search all the tourists."

"And what would we be looking for?"

Abby lifted both shoulders. "Someone could have given Bert candy laced with digitalis. Or... Maybe someone offered him a sugar substitute. You know, something like Stevia."

"And how do you think the digitalis got into the little packet?"

"Where there's a will, there's a way." To illustrate her point, she dangled the teabag. "See, the little string is held by a staple." Abby frowned. "I can't believe no one's come up with a better alternative."

"You can get them without the staple," Joshua said.

"Can you? Oh, yes you can. But then, you have to

fish it out with a spoon." She shook her head. "I'll stick to coffee. Anyway, I'm sure if someone put their mind to it, they might be able to undo the staple, open the little packet and replace the contents with a mixture that included digitalis. And, voila. The same goes for the sugar substitute. With enough care, I'm sure one could open a little satchel, replace the contents and reseal it."

Joshua tilted his head and studied her for a moment. "Did you just come up with that?"

"I'd like to take credit, but I've watched enough TV shows to know this could be done." When Joshua gave her a raised eyebrow look, she said, "What? I do extensive reading and trawling around the Internet, but I also watch TV. Are you surprised?"

"I'm surprised at the information you store in your mind."

"What can I say? You never know when all that useless information will come in handy."

"Searching for ways to kill people?" He laughed.

"My mom tried to cultivate my sense of curiosity."

"I hope you realize, the information you get on TV is not always correct. For instance, DNA testing isn't done overnight."

Abby shook her head. "Someone must know something. Someone must have noticed something." But no one had said anything because they didn't suspect foul play, she thought. "Have you made an inroad into the tourists' backgrounds?"

Frowning, Joshua tapped his watch. "It's after eleven."

"Huh?"

"Eleven in the evening."

"Oh, I hadn't realized. My goodness. Time flies when you're…" She looked down at herself. "Dressed as a cat burglar."

"Yes, I wanted to ask…"

Abby grimaced. "I'd rather you didn't."

Chapter Eight

"Working on a crime board by myself is…" Dull, Abby thought, and she'd only been at it for half an hour. "Having people around does make a difference," she told Doyle. Turning, she checked to see if he hadn't dozed off. "Oh, good. You're still awake."

Doyle gave a halfhearted wag of his tail and yawned.

"Fine. I guess you want to go to bed. Come on." She went through their little ritual of plumping up his doggy bed and sitting cross-legged beside him to tell him about her day. "You missed quite a bit today. I guess the weather makes you want to snooze. I wonder if you saw something odd. Remember, you're my star cub reporter. You need to be my eyes and ears. Although, if you did see something, how would you tell me? All right, buddy. Have a good night. I still have some work to get through."

Abby spent the next half hour standing in front of the wall looking at the photo of the tourists Faith had printed out. She then flipped through the photos on her cell phone. There had to be something she'd seen but hadn't connected to anything. Looking back up at the group photo, she studied one face and then the other.

"Did one of you go too far?" Since the name tags were barely legible, she taped several blank pieces of paper alongside the group photo and began adding names and possible reasons for wanting to see Bert dead.

"Greed. It's the only reason I can think of in this case. Okay, maybe jealousy too. Bert might have shown more interest in one woman." She tapped the pen against her chin. What if a man in the group had acted out of jealousy?

She hoped Joshua would be able to find out if any of them had received large sums of money. That would temporarily put the person in the clear since getting money now would mean they didn't have to wait for Bert to die.

Joshua had said Denise Lowe had contested the will because her dad had left money to his friends.

Abby sighed. "What if the bailout money wasn't enough? What if the person wanted to get their hands on more now rather than later?"

Staring up at the ceiling, she sighed. "Find the

motive, find the killer, and… find the proof. Yes, we need physical evidence. But where to start? I don't have the resources to research all these people."

"Social media."

"Huh?" Abby swung around. "Who said that? Hello?"

"Hi."

Abby gulped. "Mom?"

"Over here. On the coffee table."

Abby looked down at the coffee table. Her laptop… Had she left it on?

"Abby, you have some explaining to do."

$$\sim$$

Abby rose to her feet and went to answer the knock at the door.

"I came as soon as I could," Faith said and strode in. "Meaning, I swung by Joyce's for some coffee. You know what she's like. She wanted to know if I had any news." Noticing the laptop on the coffee table, Joyce whispered, "I guess we're not alone."

"No, you're not, Faith. The cat is out of the bag," her mom said. "Abby's mom… Me… knows what you two have been up to."

Faith cringed. "I hope it wasn't anything I said. Please tell me I didn't give the game away."

"Relax. You did great." Abby pointed at herself. "I had to listen to an earful from my mom last night. You'd think I would just switch the laptop off, but then I'd never hear the end of it. Come in. Make yourself at home and put on your thinking cap."

Faith looked at the wall. "I guess it's time to roll up our sleeves. I see you've been busy."

Her mom cleared her throat.

Abby smiled. "You're looking at a joint effort. We've both been busy." After her mom had given her a huge piece of her mind for trying to keep the facts about Bert's death a secret, she'd come onboard and had helped her work through the information Abby had at hand. "I've been waiting for you to show up so we can knuckle down and start throwing around some ideas. Mom?"

"Yes, Abby."

"Can you remember that first night at the pub when you waved goodnight? I saw someone in Bert's room… Sort of. Did you notice anyone missing from the group?"

"You asked me this last night, Abby."

"Yes, and you said you were going to sleep on it because when there's something troubling you, the best thing to do is to get a good night's rest."

"Are you mocking me?" her mom asked.

"Nope, I'm only wondering if your sleep yielded any results."

"I really don't want to point fingers of suspicion at someone without first being sure." Her mom looked anywhere but at Abby.

"At least give us a name and we can help you work through your ideas." Abby gave her mom a nod of encouragement.

"I've been thinking about it and I remember waving goodnight."

"Yes. And?"

"I can picture everyone sitting at the table. I probably looked at them for a couple of seconds but in that time, I remember seeing someone sitting down and someone getting up."

Abby and Faith exchanged a raised eyebrow look.

"Well, that's great, Mom. We've narrowed it all down to two persons. Who were they?"

Her mom scooped in a breath and pushed it out slowly. "Alice and Linda. Remember, I told you they both had their eyes on Bert."

"The ones who hogged the conversations?" Abby asked.

"Yes, although…" Her mom shrugged. "I wouldn't quite put it like that. Some people are more outgoing than others."

"Okay, so which one sat down and which one got up?" The person who got up might have been on their way upstairs, Abby thought.

Her mom wrung her hands. "I'm working on that."

"Is there something we can do to help you remember?" Abby asked.

"I just need to clear something in my mind because I keep seeing someone else walking toward the table and sitting down. I think it might have been someone carrying a drink so they might have gone up to the bar."

"Okay. That's good. Can you remember what they wore? We could cross reference it with the photo I took the next morning. People traveling don't carry that many sweaters. She might have worn the same one." Abby took the laptop and held it up closer to the wall so her mom could look at the group photo. "Well?"

"Cynthia. Yes. Cynthia. She had a drink in her hand and... yes, I saw her making her way to the table. I remember the flash of pale pink and thinking how some women revert to childhood colors like pink. Unfortunately, it doesn't really suit her complexion. With her coloring, she might want to try wearing brighter shades."

So, when her mom had waved goodnight, Cynthia had been on her way back to the table. Abby closed her eyes and tried to remember the scene. Clearly, she hadn't been paying that much attention. "And you say you saw her carrying a glass?"

"Yes."

Okay. She might have gone upstairs and then swung by the bar to get a drink. That actually put Cynthia in the clear because after her mom had waved goodnight, Abby had gone upstairs, and that's when she'd tried to open the wrong door. By that time, she had disconnected the video chat, so her mom couldn't confirm or deny it.

"It has to be Alice or Linda," Abby said.

"I think I should try some meditation," her mom

hummed. "If I can sit quietly for a while, it might all come back to me. Or…" Her mom clicked her fingers. "I could get pencil and paper and sketch out the scene. It might help refresh my memory."

"That's a great idea, Mom. You do that and Faith and I will take Doyle for a walk." Abby went in search of Doyle's coat but she didn't find it in its usual spot by his doggy bed. "Help me look for Doyle's tartan coat, please."

"Sure. Where do you think you put it?" Faith asked.

"It should be in the same place I always put it. By his bed." Abby looked down at Doyle. "Hey, have you seen your coat?" Doyle averted his gaze.

Faith chortled. "I get the feeling he doesn't like his coat. He must have hidden it."

"What are you talking about? He loves his coat."

"Oh, yeah? Every time you bring it out you tell him how good he looks in it but he cowers away." Faith looked under the bed. "Found it."

"Doyle. Did you hide your beautiful coat? Well, one of us has to be the grown-up. You have to wear it. It's cold outside."

"I've been thinking," Faith said. "You claim to have seen someone in Bert's room and your mom says she saw someone leave the tour group table. You were jet lagged and your mom is still trying to add authenticity to her virtual trip by turning all the clocks to Australian time so she must be sleep deprived or still adjusting to the time difference."

Abby finished buttoning up Doyle's little jacket and straightened. "Yes? Are you trying to make a point?"

"Don't take this the wrong way... You and your mom might be unreliable witnesses."

"Pardon?"

Faith shrugged. "Neither one of you can be really sure about what you saw."

Abby gave it some thought. "Yes, but... We're thinking about it. I'm not actually making any firm statements or accusations and mom wants to be sure too."

Faith tilted her head in thought. "I'm willing to accept that, but I suspect it might be viewed differently by someone in the legal profession."

"Joshua didn't have any issues. In fact, he told me off for keeping the information to myself."

"I'm only saying you should be prepared for the worst. Joshua might be happy to look into your lead, but that city detective might dismiss your suspicions as meddling. And, if he's the stickler that Joshua says he is, he might even throw the book at you for wasting valuable police time. In fact, I wouldn't be surprised if he does it just to prove that meddlesome women do not solve crimes. He's the type to think that, I'm sure."

"Exactly what type is that?" Abby asked.

"The misogynist. I've read up on them."

Abby frowned. "You've labeled him?"

Faith shrugged. "I like to keep myself entertained. Anyhow, I'd watch out for him."

"I'm only trying to do my civic duty," Abby said. "Okay. Doyle's as ready as he'll ever be. Let's go."

Faith strode out of the apartment with Abby following. As she turned to lock the door, Faith nudged her.

"Is that Cynthia standing outside Bert's room?" Faith whispered.

Abby turned. "Yes. It is."

Cynthia looked up. Seeing them, she swung away and rushed along the corridor.

"Wait," Abby called out.

"Is she actually going to pretend she didn't hear you?" Faith asked as she lunged toward Cynthia, making a grab for her before she reached the stairs.

Cynthia yelped. "What are you doing?"

"That's what we'd like to ask you," Faith said. "What were you doing outside Bert Howington's room?"

Abby caught up with them. "We only want to ask a few questions."

"Why should I talk to you?" Cynthia surprised them by asking. For a quiet woman, her voice packed quite a punch and some bite.

"Because Abby carries some weight with the police and if you can convince her of your innocence, they'll go easy on you." Faith gave a firm nod.

Abby's eyebrows rose a notch. She guessed Faith had decided to play her own version of bad cop. She plucked out the first question that came to mind and watched for Cynthia's reaction. "We only want to know if you garden." Cynthia's cheeks turned a faint shade of pink, but she had fair skin so Abby supposed that would be her reaction to anyone asking her a question.

Cynthia crossed her arms and gave a stiff nod. "As a matter of fact, yes I do."

"Aha!" Faith exclaimed.

"A few of the people in our group belong to a gardening club," Cynthia continued. "What of it?"

Abby wanted to ask if any of them grew Foxglove in their gardens but decided to leave it for Joshua to determine if it would be worth pursuing. "Why were you outside Bert's room?"

"What business is it of yours?"

Faith grinned. "She's a snoopy reporter, she makes it her business." When Cynthia didn't respond, Faith added, "Were you experiencing a fit of remorse?"

Cynthia's expression crumbled and her bottom lip wobbled. When she looked away, Abby thought she might cry. "We... We were supposed to meet today, just the two of us to talk. Traveling with the group, we rarely had time to talk alone." She gulped in a breath. "Yes. I felt remorse. Bert had wanted to talk the night before but I'd hesitated, saying it would look too obvious."

"What would look too obvious?" Abby asked.

"Leaving the others. They would have talked." She looked Abby square in the eye. "I wish I'd said yes. Now it's too late."

"Are you crossing Cynthia off your list?" Faith asked as they stepped outside the pub. "She could have been putting on an act."

Abby turned her collar up and wished she'd brought a scarf along. "Despite what you might think, I'm actually taking a backseat on this investigation. I don't want to get Joshua into trouble."

"Abby, you have a crime board in your apartment."

"It's nothing but behind the scenes prodding." Abby narrowed her eyes and pointed across the street. "Is that Alice?" She stood on the opposite sidewalk and kept looking around her. "Is she talking to herself?"

Faith lifted her hand to shield her eyes. "I think she is. Although… she might be on the phone."

"I don't see her holding one." Abby's curiosity got the better of her. She drew out her cell phone and snapped a photo. "I'm sending you another photo." As they crossed the street, a car pulled out and drove off, giving them a clear view of Alice. "She's not holding a cell."

"I'm surprised she's out here alone. Maybe that means something," Faith said when they reached the other sidewalk.

Yes, but what? "Look, there's Linda going into the café." Abby looked over her shoulder and saw Alice heading back to the pub. "That's strange. Every time I've seen them, they've been together. As thick as thieves. And both vying for Bert's attention."

"Maybe they thought of Bert as the glue that held them together," Faith suggested.

"Let's go see if Linda is meeting someone at the café." They hurried along with Doyle trotting between them. "Oh, she's alone."

"Are we going inside?" Faith asked.

Divide and conquer, Abby thought. "Yes. Let's get a table next to hers."

"I think we can be bolder than that. Let's ask if we can join her," Faith suggested.

Approaching the table, Abby saw Linda pull out a laptop from her bag. Abby nudged Faith and whispered, "She might have come here to use the wi-fi away from prying eyes." She steered Faith toward the next table but Faith insisted on the bold approach.

"Hi, mind if we join you?" Faith asked and didn't wait to be invited or told to take a hike.

Linda did mind but Faith would not be deterred so Abby drew out a chair. Giving Linda a small smile, she said, "I'm Eleanor's daughter."

"Yes, I know. I also know you're the local reporter. I've already talked to the police and I have nothing to add."

Joshua had spoken to the tourists? "Did the police single you out or did they interview everyone?"

"They lined us up like the usual suspects. I've never been so insulted."

That didn't sound like Joshua. "When did this happen?"

"Yesterday afternoon," Linda blurted out. "We were all hauled to the police station. The younger detective was polite enough but the other one…" Linda shivered. "Rude. Brusque. Impatient. Now, instead of fond memories of this trip, I'm going to have nightmares about being interrogated. I have a good mind to lodge a complaint."

The police had questioned them in the afternoon? That must have been when she'd taken Doyle for a walk and found Mitch in the alley. Abby looked at Faith who mouthed an apology because she'd obviously missed it all too.

Abby was about to ask another question when Linda's words registered in her mind. She had fond memories of the trip? Had she forgotten about Bert dying? Had it been a careless slip? According to her mom, Linda had been keen on Bert. Maybe she had been pretending.

"What did the police want to know?" Abby asked.

Linda clammed up.

"I bet anything they wanted to know about your financial situation," Faith said.

Linda's cheeks reddened slightly.

"Let me guess," Faith continued, "You're in debt up to your eyeballs and could do with a windfall."

"You two have a nerve coming in here to harass me." Linda grabbed her laptop and surged to her feet. Doyle just managed to scramble out of her way as she stormed off.

"I think my interrogation skills could do with some improvement," Faith said. "Are suspects usually so uncooperative with you?"

"You did sort of come across as a bull in a china shop." Abby grinned. "Next time, you might want to ease into it by being more suggestive. Lead up to the question. Make it sound conversational, as if a thought just occurred to you."

Faith looked around the café. "I don't see any other tourists. Should we hunt them down?"

"Do I need to put a leash on you?" Abby checked her cell phone and winced. "Mom's been sending me text messages. I actually forgot about her." Abby checked the wi-fi at the café and connected her mom.

"As I said, social media," her mom said.

"Hi, Mom."

"You girls need to do your research. Most of the tourists have private accounts but a couple of them have public ones and they've shared their gardening club photos. Linda and Cynthia are cottage garden enthusiasts and they both planted Foxgloves last summer. We shouldn't jump to conclusions because anyone in the group might have harvested the plant for their nefarious purposes."

Abby and Faith stared at each other, their eyes not blinking.

"Nefarious," Faith mouthed.

"Alice excels at growing herbs," her mom continued. "Do you know what that means?"

"Not really." Abby didn't even try to figure it out.

"She knows how to dry herbs. One of the gardeners posted a photo of Alice in her garden shed with bunches of herbs hanging off the ceiling. I daresay, she knows the process inside and out. That makes her a likely candidate for your suspect list."

"I'll mention it to Joshua but I know he'll want to find hard evidence of Alice's abilities. As well as motive. Why would she want to kill Bert? He'd bailed her out."

"You worry too much about motive," her mom said. "I'm willing to bet anything the killer has a feeble excuse for committing the crime. Also, you've been concentrating on the women. What if it's one of the men, jealous because of all the attention Bert got or because he won all that money. It's enough for someone to think something isn't fair for them to go and do something drastic like commit murder."

"Your mom has a point. We haven't spent any time thinking about the men. Why's that?"

Abby didn't need to look down at the cell phone to see her mom looking at her with a lifted eyebrow. "Interesting question. I guess this is all about assuming men are more likely to bludgeon someone to death than…" Abby sat back. "Commit to a lengthy process of slowly poisoning someone," she finished. "The person responsible took their time. For all we know, they might have been giving Bert small doses of digitalis over a long time." That could be confirmed by his medical records and the lab report. If he had been complaining of fatigue for a while, then her theory would fall into place.

"Going by the posts online," her mom said, "They all live within a few miles of each other and keep in regular touch. In fact, they take turns to host weekly get-togethers."

"Okay. So, we're probably looking for someone who used to see Bert every day." Abby tried to picture one of the women offering Bert a cupcake laced with digitalis...

"His daughter," Faith said.

Yes, quite possibly, Abby thought. Denise Lowe had run his household. She would have had access to his medication, but that had already been tested. "There's still the question of how the killer managed to sneak the deadly digitalis into Bert."

Chapter Nine

*W*hile Faith went to the office to print out more photos for their crime collage, Abby tried to coax Doyle into walking around the block but with every step he took he cast a longing look over his shoulder. "All right, I'll put you out of your misery, but I swear, if you gain weight, you're going on a diet."

At the pub, Abby removed his tartan coat and watched Doyle scurry toward his spot by the fireplace. "Don't go wandering off," she teased, "I'm taking your coat upstairs." She sniffed it. "Either your coat needs a wash or it's bath time for you." Doyle curled up into a tight ball. "Hey, you like your pampering time. Katherine makes you smell lovely."

Rushing up the stairs, she swerved in time to avoid colliding with a man coming down. Abby didn't remember seeing him at the pub. He carried a suitcase and looked to be in a bad mood.

"Watch where you're going," a familiar voice snapped.

Abby looked up and straight into an angry face.

Denise Lowe.

The man with the suitcase had to be the husband, Abby thought.

Goodbye and good riddance. She continued on her way. As she strode by Bert's room, she noticed the door had been left ajar. Before she could change her mind, Abby drew out her second cell phone and went in to take some more photos so she could have before and after shots of the room.

Out of curiosity, she checked to see if Denise Lowe had helped herself to the complimentary soap and shampoo.

She had!

She'd even taken the tea bags and coffee. "My goodness. She even took the towels."

Abby was about to leave when she noticed a small basket lined with a plastic bag under the table. Had Joshua checked the trash?

He must have. Surely, he had...But, what if he'd missed something? She knew the room hadn't been cleaned since Bert's death...

Bending down, Abby saw something in the bottom of the basket. "Hello, what do we have here? The proof we need? A solid lead?" She reached for it, but before she could fish it out, everything went dark.

～

"She's still breathing. Abby, can you hear me?"

"Check for gun wounds."

"Why would I do that? Did you hear a gunshot?"

"No, but the killer might have had a silencer."

"You've been watching too many cop shows."

"She's moaning. That has to be a good sign."

"Yeah, keep talking and she'll keep moaning."

Too many voices, Abby thought. And why were they all yelling?

"She's opening her eyes."

Abby groaned.

"See what you've done now. She went from moaning to groaning."

"The ambulance is on its way. Stay with us, Abby."

"Where do you think she's going to go? She's limp."

Abby felt her arm being lifted and released. It flopped and landed with a soft thud so she did the only thing she could do. She growled.

～

"Hello," a deep but friendly voice said.

Abby tried to swallow. Her throat felt so dry… "Hi."

"Do you remember what happened?"

"Who are you?" Abby asked. Her words sounded slurred. Had she fallen asleep? She opened her eyes but immediately closed them. "Ouch. Would you mind not pointing that light straight into my eyes?"

"Sorry. I have to check your reflexes. You had a nasty blow to your head. We're going to play it safe and take you for a ride to the hospital."

"Oh, no. No. No. I'm fine." To prove it, she tried to sit up but the entire room moved right along with her. "Okay, that would be nice. I could do with a vacation. Oh, wait. I've just come back from one. Actually, I need to get to work. I have an article to write…"

"Maybe tomorrow."

~

"There's no need for you to worry about your mom finding out. I told her you have a serious case of the runs. So, you're not feeling your best." Faith plumped up Abby's pillow. "There, that's better."

"Thank you, Faith. You're a good nurse."

"My parents wanted me to go into nursing but I've never been keen on wearing a uniform."

"Hang on… You told my mom I have the what?"

"The runs." Faith shrugged. "You know, diarrhea."

"Huh?"

"I know. I was embarrassed for you, but I used that to our advantage. I told your mom you'd rather not talk about it. Anyhow, it didn't surprise your mom. After all, you have been pigging out since you arrived." Faith grinned. "I didn't want her pointing an accusatory finger at Hannah's food or Joyce's café, so I told her all that food you'd been eating had taken its toll and backed you up a bit. That's when you took matters into your own hands and self-medicated with laxatives. I told her you misread the instructions and ended up taking too much. I threw in a slight case of dehydration, just to be safe, and voila. You're in hospital and she is none the wiser." Faith grinned. "As per our modus operandi, everyone's been put on notice. There's to be no mention of you being attacked and hit on the head."

Abby tried to sit up. "How long have I been here?"

"Overnight. The doctor said you're good to go so I brought you a change of clothes."

Abby raked her fingers through her hair and winced. She had a serious bump on the back of her head. "What happened?"

"We've been trying to put the pieces together…"

"We?"

"Mitch, Markus and me. They were both first on the scene after Doyle alerted them. He's such a good boy. Doyle jumped to his feet and started barking. When he got Markus' attention, he took off up the stairs. So, technically, he found you first. Anyhow, when they reached the room, you were out for the count. Mitch thought you'd been shot, but Markus figured that couldn't be the case because no one had heard a shot. At about the same time, I'd finished printing the photos so I made my way to your apartment and that's when I came across Mitch and Markus arguing and discussing the fact that you'd gone from moaning to groaning and then onto growling. The ambulance arrived and here you are."

"Okay. So, what happened to me?" Abby frowned. "I think I just asked that."

"Oh, well... We're sure someone hit you on the head. Can you remember what you were doing in Bert's room?"

"I... I must have had a reason for going in there."

"The doctor mentioned you might suffer temporary amnesia or a feeling of disorientation." Faith gave her a bright smile. "But it'll all come back to you. I'm sure the moment you set foot inside the pub everything will look familiar and trigger something."

What if it didn't?

"At least we know the killer is still among us," Faith said.

"Is that supposed to make me feel better?"

"Come on, let's get you dressed and out of here. Joshua is waiting for us outside. Brace yourself, I left him drumming his fingers on the steering wheel so he's going to give you a lecture."

~

"You need to keep hydrated, Abby."

It took a moment for Abby to remember Faith had told her mom she had taken an overdose of laxatives. "Yes, Mom."

"I don't understand what you were so embarrassed

about. It happens. I'm your mother. You should have told me."

"I'll remember that for next time, Mom." If only she could remember what she'd been doing in Bert's room. Had something caught her attention? She'd already had a look inside and had even taken photos. She glanced over at the wall to see if the pictures could trigger something in her mind. Maybe in time... but she didn't have time.

"So, while you were otherwise occupied," her mom said, "I did some more research. Let me check my notes. I'll be back in a sec."

As Abby waited for her mom to organize herself, she hugged Doyle against her and gave him a scratch under his chin. "You're my hero." Abby's stomach grumbled. Sliding to the edge of the chair, she whispered, "I'm going downstairs to get some food."

Faith shook her head. "Order in. Joshua couldn't spare any officers. If you set foot outside the apartment, he'll skin me alive. I'm under strict orders to keep you here. Consider yourself under house arrest." Faith grinned. "For your own good."

Abby looked around but didn't see her cell phone anywhere. "Where did you put my cell?"

Faith signaled to the one on the coffee table.

"My other cell," Abby mouthed.

Faith's shoulder rose a notch. "I... I'm not sure."

Abby used the landline to place an order for room service. When Mitch answered, she asked him if he'd seen her cell phone. When she'd walked into Bert's room, she had been holding it in her hand and, since he'd come to her rescue, he might have seen it.

"Nope. How are you feeling this morning?" Mitch asked.

"Great. Can you ask Markus about my cell, please?" Abby rubbed the back of her head. It still felt tender. Had her assailant taken her cell? "Oh, and send up some food, please. A burger with the lot and some fries. Actually, lots of fries."

"Are you sure that's what you want? Considering your recent experience with the runs, you might want to take it easy and have a steak."

If anything, Abby thought, the people of Eden knew how to play their designated roles to the hilt. "If I insist on a burger, will I get one?"

"Probably not. At The Gloriana, we make customer service our top priority and that includes looking after the welfare of our guests. Also, your mom called earlier to say you need to play it safe and have a steak."

She ended the call and drew Faith aside, away from her mom's hearing. "You'll have to get me another cell phone." Abby bit the edge of her lip. "My attacker must have taken it."

"Why?" Faith asked.

"I have no idea. Let's run through what we did before I came back to the pub."

"We saw Alice." Faith clicked her fingers. "You took a photo of her." Rushing to the coffee table, Faith pulled a photo out of a stack and showed her. "You sent it to me so I could print it."

Had Abby given someone reason to want to steal her cell phone?

Faith leaned in and whispered, "Your attacker must have taken the phone because he… or she either thought you had some sort of proof in your phone or they didn't want you coming to and calling for help."

"No, that can't be it. If they wanted me out of the way, they would have hit me harder." Abby's eyes widened. Someone had tried to kill her or get her out of the way. She strode across the room toward the window. Had Alice noticed her taking a photo? What if she had? Alice had been standing on the sidewalk, talking to herself. "Can I see that photo again, please?" Alice had been standing beside a car. The words echoed in her mind. "When we crossed the street, that car took off."

"Oh, it's coming back to you," Faith said. "That probably means you're on the mend."

"Yes, but… We assumed Alice had been talking to herself. What if she'd been talking to someone in the car?"

"When in doubt, better call Joshua." As Faith pressed her cell to her ear, she squinted and tried to read the license plate. "Hello, detective. Abby wants to talk with you."

Abby settled back down on the couch.

"What happened to you taking it easy?" Joshua asked. "You promised you would."

"Someone hit me on the head. This is personal now, and they stole my cell phone. We're thinking they might have wanted to get their hands on a photo I took. I'm having the last laugh because we have the photo. Can you run the plates for us?"

"Because…"

"Well, we think Alice might have been talking with someone. What if she had a clandestine rendezvous with a co-conspirator?"

"In the middle of town and in plain view of everyone?" Joshua asked and, knowing Abby would persevere, he added, "What's the number?"

"I'll get Faith to send you a copy of the photo. You might have to magnify the shot. I'll talk to you later. My lunch is here." Abby opened the door and smacked her lips.

Mitch strode in and set the tray on the table. Looking at the laptop, he mouthed, "Is it safe?"

"Yes, my mom's organizing her notes, but we should still tread with care, so keep your voice down."

"Have you made any headway?" Mitch asked.

Shaking her head, Abby said, "My cell is still missing and so is most of my memory of yesterday. Every time I think I've retrieved something, I second guess myself. I know I came into the pub so my mind automatically goes through what I normally do."

"And what do you think that is?" Mitch asked.

"Make my way to the bar." Doyle stretched and yawned. "Hang on. I took Doyle's jacket off." Then, she'd made her way upstairs. "Hey. I nearly crashed into someone. A man. He had a suitcase."

Mitch brushed his hand across his chin. "And?"

"And... I've never seen him before. Oh, I then saw Denise Lowe. She looked angry." Abby pumped her fist in the air. "Yes. I remember feeling relieved because I thought we'd be seeing the last of her. Please tell me she's gone for good."

Mitch nodded. "She got the go-ahead from the police and came to clear out her dad's belongings."

"Did she come alone?"

"Her husband came with her."

That must have been the man she'd seen.

"Eat up or your food will get cold."

"Where's my lunch?" Faith asked.

"Sorry," Abby said around a mouthful of steak. "The blow to my head must have blocked out my manners. I only ordered for myself."

"Blow to your head?" her mom asked. "What blow? Abby, have you been lying to me again?"

~

"Technically, you didn't lie to your mom. I did," Faith said. "And you have to admit, I came up with a rock-solid explanation."

"Yes, how clumsy of me to have knocked my head when I bent down to retrieve Doyle's coat from under the bed. Nice job thinking on your feet." Abby knew she also had her mom's neighbor to thank for the reprieve. She'd dropped in for a cup of coffee just as Abby's mom had been about to launch into a full-scale reprimand for keeping the real facts hidden from her.

Abby skimmed through the notes her mom had sent her. She had been busy. "Bert's son has money problems. He's been declared bankrupt. That's definitely motive for murder." But he hadn't been anywhere near Eden.

"How did she get that information?" Faith asked. "She's all the way over in the States."

"The wonders of the internet," Abby mused. "She made a note of her thinking process and listed money as a main motivator for murder. She then found a database listing bankrupts. It's called the BRS, which sounds like an acronym for a swear word. Anyhow, it searches the national personal insolvency index. That's a permanent record of personal insolvencies in Australia. I guess this is the modern version of debtors' prison." Seeing Faith's vacant expression, Abby went on to add, "In the 1800s, debtors' prisons were a common way of dealing with unpaid debt."

"I'm lucky my folks taught me to live within my means," Faith said. "If I want something, I have to save up for it."

"Yes, well. Instant gratification is the modern-day plague. We want things now. But it's not always about overspending. Some people who declare themselves bankrupt usually have a business that went belly up."

Abby stretched her legs. Since returning from hospital, she'd done nothing but sit down. "I need to go out for a walk."

"You're supposed to rest and take it easy," Faith said. "I promised your mom I'd take care of you. You don't have to lift a finger. Everything is taken care of. Even the cleaning."

Abby sat up. "I think I just remembered something." She got on the phone and called Markus. When he picked up, she asked, "Did the maid clean Bert's room the morning he died?"

"No, she was running late and then the police asked me to make sure no one went in."

"So, when's the last time she cleaned the room?"

"This morning."

So, whatever she thought she saw had now been cleaned away or it had been taken by her attacker. Not that it mattered since she knew Joshua had done a thorough search of the room. She couldn't possibly think he'd missed something. "While I have you on the line, could you send up some coffee, please?"

"I thought Mitch had gone up," Markus said.

"Yes, and then I got into trouble with my mom so he beat a hasty retreat."

"What's going through your mind?" Faith asked.

Abby disconnected the call and sat back. "I'm entertaining a couple of thoughts. Firstly, I'm wondering if Denise Lowe removed something the police missed when she came to collect her dad's belongings. She would have known what to look for." Abby rubbed the tender spot on her head. "Secondly, I think I bent down to pick something up." She must have had her back to the door. Had she been followed upstairs?

Who would have seen her going upstairs?

"Let's add a few names to the crime board," Abby suggested. "I need to remember everyone I saw when I came into the pub." She surged to her feet but her legs crumbled beneath her. "Whoa. Dizzy."

~

"What happened?" Abby tried to sit up but it felt too comfortable lying down.

"You sort of fainted but you came to straight away and then you curled up on the couch and fell asleep. I called the doctor and he told me to keep you awake."

"How exactly did you do that?" Abby asked and rubbed her cheek.

"I tapped you on the cheek." Faith grinned. "Okay, I sort of slapped you. Hey, needs must. You suffered a possible concussion. You're not supposed to fall asleep."

Faith rose to her feet and went to answer the door. "Oh, good. Coffee. Abby needs to stay awake."

Markus strode in and looked around the sitting room. "Is it safe to talk?"

"My mom's having coffee with her neighbor. At least, I think she is."

Faith checked the laptop. "Yes. She's off-line."

"Okay," Markus said. "I brought you enough coffee to stave off fatigue. You're in luck because this is a state of the art dosage."

"Huh?"

"It's been scientifically proven," Markus quirked his eyebrows up. "There's even an algorithm." He pointed at the mug of coffee. "This is a 200 milligrams or 3.5 ounces serving. That should keep you going for an hour. I'll bring another one in an hour's time."

"Three and a half ounces? What's the usual serving?" Abby asked.

Markus gave her a lopsided grin. "Half that. This is bound to keep you upright for a while." Markus set aside some cushions and sat down. "Has anything come back to you?"

Abby wanted to shake her head but decided against any sudden movements. "I'm trying to remember everyone I saw when I walked into the pub. The killer might have been sitting at the bar."

"Okay. I might be able to help," Markus said. "I'd been in the dining room and I walked into the bar. That's when I saw you going up the stairs."

"Great." Abby perked up. "Did you see Denise Lowe coming down the stairs with her husband?"

Markus clasped his hands. "Her husband? No, I didn't see him. I saw her brother."

"Huh?"

He nodded. "When she arrived earlier, she made a

beeline for the stairs. So, I stopped her." Markus grinned. "I knew she'd come to clear out her dad's stuff, but I couldn't miss the opportunity to annoy her. The woman is made of steel. To be honest with you, I don't think she cares about her dad's death. Some people excel at hiding their feelings, she doesn't have any."

"How can you be sure?" Abby asked.

"I watch and listen. I've been doing it all my life. Easy enough to do when you grow up in a pub. I know you all think she's been hiding her emotions, but some people just don't have any to hide. Anyway, long story short, I pretended I didn't know her and said I couldn't allow just anyone to waltz in as if they owned the place."

Abby rubbed her eyes. "Okay. Tell me about the man with her."

"Oh, since I'd never seen him before, I subjected him to a security check. I actually made him produce his driver's license. He didn't like that. His name is Robert Howington." Markus grinned.

"So, why did Mitch think he was her husband?"

Markus gave her a lift of his eyebrows and drawled out, "I told you. I dropped him on his head when he was a baby."

Slumping down on the couch, Abby sighed.

"I think she's having a relapse," Markus said.

"No, I'm not." Abby straightened. "So, what happened next?"

"They went upstairs and I went back to the dining room."

Meaning, he'd gone back to the kitchen to be with Hannah. "What about the tourists? When we left the pub, they weren't there."

"Yeah, they came back and sat at the bar. Just don't ask me to name them. I know they have those ridiculous name tags pinned on but one of the women caught me trying to read it and gave me a pursed lip look. She must have thought I'd been looking at something else." He bobbed his eyebrows up and down. "If you get my meaning."

Faith retrieved the photo from the wall and held it up in front of Markus. "Can you point to them?"

"They were all there, except that one."

Faith leaned down to look at the person he'd pointed at. "Linda. Yes, we saw her at the café."

"And that one."

"Alice," Faith said. "We saw her outside. But when we headed to the café, we saw her coming back to the pub."

"She might have gone in the residents' entrance," Markus suggested and then he pointed to another person.

"Steph."

"Steph wasn't there?" Abby drew down her brow. "Has she come up in conversation?"

Markus chuckled. "Are you two about to point the

finger of suspicion her way because she escaped your notice?"

Steph hadn't said or done anything to raise their suspicions. In fact, if Abby had to be honest with herself, she had no idea who the culprit might be. If she had to suspect someone of hitting her on the head...

Alice? If she'd gone back inside the pub via the residents' entrance, she might have gone straight upstairs to her room. A few scenarios ran through Abby's mind. Alice could have heard Abby. She might have nudged her door open, taken and peek and then decided to take action. She might even have been inside Bert's room. When she heard someone coming up, she might have hurried out and hidden around a corner...

"Did you see Denise Lowe go upstairs again?" Abby asked.

"Nope. After I saw you go up, I walked away. Mitch would have been at the bar then. Ask him." He checked his watch. "In fact, I have to go relieve him from bar duty. I'll send him up."

"Thanks, Markus."

Unfortunately, they were out of luck. Mitch swore he'd been at the bar and hadn't seen Denise Lowe go up the stairs again. In fact, he hadn't seen anyone go up the stairs.

If most of the tourists had been downstairs and Denise and her brother had left, who'd attacked her? Steph? Alice? Maybe even Linda.

"I need to get out of here and Doyle needs to go out too." Abby got his little tartan coat and put it on him. Doyle gave her a half-hearted wag of his tail and hung his head in resignation. "If you don't like your coat, we can get another one." Doyle gave her a lick on the chin. "Is that it? You don't like the color? But dogs are colorblind."

"Maybe you should get a plain colored one. Something in blue," Faith suggested.

"Yeah, I might do that. Hey… I remember I had the coat with me. How did it get here?"

"Oh, I picked it up," Faith said. "I know what you're thinking. No, I didn't see your phone. If I had, I would have picked it up."

"Okay. Let's go out the residents' door, it's closer." Abby gasped. "The residents' door. That has to be how my assailant came in." But it didn't make sense. Why would Alice hit her on the head? She couldn't be the killer. Bert had bailed her out.

Yes, but…

She knew all about drying herbs. The knowledge could have been employed to process the digitalis…

Chapter Ten

Faith gave a slow shake of her head. "It can't be Alice."

"Faith, you've spent half an hour saying that, but you haven't provided any supporting evidence to back your objection." Abby took Doyle's coat off and ran a brush through him. "Oh, you like that. Yes, who's my good doggie. You're so gorgeous."

"My reasoning is floating around my head. I have to pluck it out. Give me another minute." Faith slumped down on the couch and covered her eyes. A moment later, she sprung upright. "I've got it. We assume the killer hit you on the head."

"Yes."

"Okay. We also assume, and rightly so, the killer is responsible for somehow making sure Bert took his regular dosage of digitalis."

"That's right."

"Well, all along, you've been saying you saw someone in Bert's room the first day you arrived back in town."

"Yes."

"So, if the killer is responsible for hitting you on the head and planting the digitalis in Bert's room, then it can't be Alice because your mom said she saw her sitting with the group that first night."

Abby tapped her chin. "Oh. You're right."

"See, I'm not just a pretty face."

"Maybe she didn't act alone," Abby said and went to answer a knock at the door.

"We ran the number plates," Joshua said as he strode into Abby's apartment. "The car belongs to Denise Lowe's brother."

Faith pumped the air. "Yes."

"And?" Abby asked.

"According to him, he drove into town to give his sister moral support and to help her pack their dad's belongings."

"He didn't exactly look happy about it." Abby gave a slow shake of her head. "No. I don't like coincidences. We saw Alice standing by his car." There had to be a connection. She knew Alice would have a key to the residents' entrance. Had she opened the door for Robert Howington? Frowning, Abby strode to the window and imagined Robert Howington taking his dad's suitcase out to the car. Along the way, he contacted Alice and asked her to let him in the residents' entrance. He came up, found Abby snooping around in his dad's room and decided to get her out of the way.

"Alice had known Bert for a long time," Joshua reasoned. "I think we can safely assume she met his son at some point. Think about it. If you lose a family member who's been traveling around with a group of people, one of them might stop you to offer their condolences."

Abby exchanged a look with Faith that spoke of silent agreement. "We both got the impression she didn't want to be seen talking to him. That's why at first we thought she'd been on the phone or talking to herself."

"Unless you can read lips and know what she'd been talking about, I don't have anything to connect them. Despite what you might think, the police can't go around badgering people just because they stand in a street corner talking to themselves."

"Did you know Robert Howington is a bankrupt?" Abby asked. "That makes him desperate for money and desperate people make bad decisions and wrong choices." Abby gave a firm nod. "Also, you need to canvas the area and find out if anyone saw someone coming in through the residents' door. I'm sure that's how my assailant came in." Abby shivered. She had no trouble imagining Robert Howington coming back inside because... because he'd seen her taking the photograph. Yes, that's it, Abby thought. "You should at least check to make sure he's left. For all we know, he's still hanging around town, waiting to finish me off."

"Anything else?" Joshua asked, his eyes brimming with amusement.

Abby read the notes she'd been taking in case her memory failed her. "Yes. When I went into Bert's room, I think I saw something in the waste basket."

"We did a thorough sweep of the room, Abby."

Abby looked up at the photos Faith had taped to the wall. "You said you took samples of the tea and coffee."

"We did."

"Were there any used teabags in the waste basket?" Seeing one would have prompted her to have a closer look.

"We took samples of the tea," Joshua confirmed. "And the tests came back negative. No traces of digitalis were found."

Abby fought the urge to surge to her feet because the last time she'd tried to get up too quickly, she'd collapsed. "But you didn't test all the teabags. What if only some of them were tampered with? We're looking at a pre-meditated crime. Someone went to a lot of trouble to make sure Bert succumbed to a heart attack. And I bet anything they didn't act alone."

Joshua got up. "I'm glad you're feeling better."

"You're leaving?"

"As per your instructions, I have to go canvas the area."

~

"You'll get us into trouble, Abby."

"Just drive." She'd called the owner of Rosebud Cottage, the bed & breakfast where Denise Lowe had been staying at, and the owner, Glenda Stephens, had told her Denise hadn't left yet.

Faith grumbled. "Do you even have a plan?"

"Yes. I'm going to be confrontational."

"And where do you think that will get you?" Faith asked.

"Denise Lowe has to have a breaking point. Push her hard enough and she might make a mistake and say something to incriminate herself or someone else."

"When did we start suspecting Denise Lowe?"

"If we haven't, we should have. She had the run of the place. For all we know, she might have spoon-fed her dad the digitalis." While he'd been at home, Abby reasoned. But then, he'd gone on vacation. Had Denise Lowe engaged the services of a co-conspirator to do the dirty work for her?

"Yes, but… Why do we have to confront her?"

Abby gave a small shrug. "I don't answer to anyone, so I'm free to ask the tough questions."

"She could lodge a harassment suit against you," Faith warned. "Then you'll be answering to the law."

"Nonsense. She's guilty of something. She has to be."

"Yes, of having a mean temper and unfriendly

disposition." Faith shifted in her seat and tightened her hold on the steering wheel. "Something tells me I'm going to live to regret this."

Doyle clambered up onto Abby's lap and looked Abby in the eye. "What? Do you have something to say?"

"If Doyle could talk, I'm sure he'd be asking you to rethink your tactics," Faith said.

Abby hadn't been entirely truthful with Faith. Yes, she wanted to see how far she could push Denise Lowe. Everyone had a breaking point. Most importantly, she wanted to see how her brother would react.

He hadn't left town. Joshua had sent her a text message confirming it.

They pulled up outside Rosebud Cottage. "Looks like we nearly missed them." Denise Lowe stood on the front porch, a suitcase next to her, her attention on her cell phone.

Faith tapped her finger on the steering wheel. "Here's an idea. If Joshua checked everyone's phone records, I bet anything he'd come up with a connection. It always worked for Jessica Fletcher in Murder, She Wrote."

Abby heard her cell phone ringing. She drew both out and held them up. When Faith laughed, Abby said, "What? They both have the same ring tone." She answered her second cell. "Detective. What can I do for you?"

"You could tell me where you are," Joshua said.

"Getting some fresh air."

Joshua sighed. "I know you've been restless, so I wanted to let you know I canvassed the area and no one noticed anything unusual. I also followed the trail of the missing teabag."

"I'm listening."

"Nothing. Came up empty."

"I know what I saw," Abby insisted. At least, she thought she'd seen a teabag. "I think you've just confirmed my assailant's motive. They followed me, saw that I was about to find the teabag, they hit me over the head and made off with the teabag and my cell. That teabag might have been the one that delivered the fatal dosage."

"According to the pathologist, the digitalis had been delivered in small doses over time," Joshua explained. "One teabag is not going to cut it. We've tested the ones we found and they were free of any foreign substances. That means there's a hole in your theory."

"What about the person I saw in his room the night before he died. He or she might have gone in to remove the evidence."

"Why?"

"Because… Because maybe they knew his time was coming to an end." Abby rubbed her brow. "For all we know, Bert might have been drinking some other tea. A special blend supplied by one of his friends. My mom said Bert had complained of fatigue. If she heard him, then someone else did too and must have realized their efforts had finally paid off."

"All right. I'm starting to like the sound of that."

"You should try coming down hard on someone," Abby suggested. "Try Alice. If she knows something, she'll talk. Tell her you're onto her. Tell her you have proof she colluded with Bert's son."

"Whoa. I thought we'd been over that," Joshua said.

"Yeah, well… I'm not convinced. And I don't believe he came up here to give his sister moral support. I think he came to make sure all the evidence disappears."

"Abby."

"Yes?"

"Will you promise to stay out of trouble?"

"Of course. I have to go now." Abby unbuckled her seat belt and turned to Faith. "Ready?"

Pushing out a breath, Faith nodded. "I guess now I know how a foot soldier feels, blindly following their commander. Out of curiosity, am I getting hazard pay?"

"I thought you'd be pleased to accompany me. You always complain about having to stay behind at the office and missing out on all the excitement."

Faith hummed. "She doesn't look pleased to see us."

"How can you tell? She hasn't changed her expression." Denise Lowe's mouth was set in a grim line and lifted slightly to suggest a sneer and her cheeks appeared to be sucked in.

"My heart's pumping hard against my chest. Is that normal?" Faith asked.

"Don't worry, once the adrenaline kicks in, you'll be fine and ready for battle."

"Do you have your kid gloves on? I'm sure the situation calls for them," Faith said.

"Yes, of course. We wouldn't want to incite her wrath."

"I think you're misleading me. A moment ago, you said you were going to confront her."

"Come on, this is your chance to prove your mettle." Abby strode up to the front stoop.

"You. What are you doing here?" Denise Lowe snapped.

"I'm performing my civic duty." Abby lifted her chin. "I wanted you to know your dad enjoyed his final days surrounded by friends..."

Denise snorted. "Is this some sort of macabre last-ditch attempt to sweeten me up and let your mom have the drawing? You're all vultures. Circling around. I won't have any of it. You'll all be hearing from my lawyer."

"As I was trying to say, your dad spent his last days enjoying himself and living life to the full. But since you want to talk about last wills and testaments, I'll happily go along. You ran your dad's household. You knew everything about his comings and goings. You knew he'd planned on bequeathing money to his friends."

Denise's eyes hardened and she pursed her lips.

Abby tilted her head. "I'm thinking you wanted to put a stop to it all, but you knew your dad very well. He might have allowed you to organize things for him, but when it came to financial matters, the buck stopped with him." Abby's wild guess about Bert's character failed to have the desired effect. Abby watched for a reaction but Denise's face had turned to steel. "He'd been an accountant his entire life, keeping track of every penny. Suddenly, there he was, with more money than he knew what to do with. To your horror, he started splurging it around." Abby put her foot on the first step. "You had to put an end to it before he gave it all away."

Denise leaned down and sneered at her. "You have no idea what you're talking about. I knew he wanted to share his winnings with his friends by going on a trip and, for your information, I also knew he'd named his friends in his will." Denise shrugged. "He left everyone some money but the bulk of it goes to his family."

"Then why contest the will?"

"You should ask those vultures he called his friends. He paid for the trip, but he also gave them loans. Loans which had to be paid back. My dad's generosity had limits."

Abby frowned. "Really? You expect me to believe that? Your dad planned on leaving you some money, but not all of it. In fact, he wanted to change the will." Abby went for broke and pulled another fabricated lie out of the hat. "He'd already made an appointment with his attorney." To her surprise, Denise blanched.

Faith whispered, "Are we sitting ducks out here? I feel someone has us in their sights. Please tell me we're not about to be shot."

Faith's concerns were not unfounded. Abby sensed someone watching them too. They'd already taken enough risks. "You know what? I tried to be nice. I thought perhaps you might be in the midst of having a delayed reaction to your dad's passing. But I see there might be something to everything I've said, so I'm going to pass the information onto the police and let them handle it."

Abby swung around and, grabbing a hold of Faith's arm, she strode back to the car saying, "There's nothing wrong with a cowardly retreat." Doyle was the first one to jump in the car. "There's a good boy."

Once they were back on the road, Faith pushed out a breath. "That felt like a close call. I think you got to Denise. Question is, what will she do now?"

"I think Denise will simply go home."

"Really? Surely she must realize the police will listen to you and turn her life inside and out until they get to the bottom of her involvement."

"Yeah, I actually think her brother is the one who'll be trying to tunnel a way out." She drew out her cell and called Joshua. "Before you growl at me, can I just say I meant well."

"What did you do?" Joshua asked.

"I tried to push a few buttons."

~

They drove back to the pub in silence. When Faith's cell beeped, she asked Abby to check the message. "It's my mom. She sent an attachment. Why is she sending you things?"

"She knows I'm the one who runs to the office to print things out."

"Oh, right. Smart thinking. Okay, she's obviously been busy researching. I guess you have to swing by the newspaper and do some more printing."

"I'll drop you off at Joyce's," Faith said. "You look as if you need another shot of caffeine."

Abby rubbed her temple. "Yes. I think I do. I'm experiencing a post-adrenaline rush slump."

"Joyce will perk you up in no time."

Faith's cell beeped again. "It's my mom, again. She wants to connect." Abby drew out her second cell phone. Frowning, she looked at Faith. "What if the killer didn't act alone? How did they communicate with their accomplice?"

"Only one way to know for sure. As I said, Jessica Fletcher would check the phone records. How about you go in and have your coffee?" Faith suggested. "I'll send Joshua a text message asking him to look into every-one's phone records. I'd like to see if I have any influ-ence over him."

When Faith stopped the car outside the café, Abby slid out and adjusted Doyle's coat. "We don't want you catching a chill. Come on. The wind has some bite. Let's go inside."

Striding in, she almost collided with Joyce who stood waiting for her, her arms crossed, her expression serious.

"You've chased my customers away," Joyce growled.

Abby looked around the café. There were only a couple of tables free. "What are you talking about? The place is buzzing."

"The tourists. They've stayed away all day. I had to call Mitch to find out if they were still in town."

Abby settled down at a table and set up the video chat. "Say hello to my mom."

Joyce fixed a smile in place and waved to her mom. "How are you enjoying your stay in our quiet little town, Eleanor?"

"Oh, give it up, Joyce. I know all about Bert being killed."

"Heavens," Joyce exclaimed. "Killed? How? When?"

Chapter Eleven

*C*rossing the street, Abby met Faith.

"What are you so happy about?" Faith asked.

Abby smiled. "For once, Joyce was late with the news. She had no idea my mom knew about the murder. Oh, and look. We've been shopping. Doyle has a new coat in royal blue." An hour away from her apartment had been enough to clear Abby's head. She had no business getting involved in murder investigations. In a few days, her mom's virtual tour would be over and Abby could go back to work. By then, Joshua would have made an arrest. The truth had to come out, eventually.

"Where is your mom?" Faith asked.

"I left her at Joyce's café. She's making the rounds, getting to know the locals." They avoided the bar and went in the residents' entrance. "What's this?" Abby asked as she noticed the piece of paper Faith held.

Faith waved it and smiled. "It's the attachment your mom sent. I printed it out. It's a drawing." They strode into Abby's apartment and Faith made a beeline for the wall and added the drawing to their collage. "You know how she'd been trying to remember which tourist was missing from the group the night before Bert died? Well, she put pencil to paper. I think she did a great job capturing their likenesses. Anyway, she circled a name. Steph. While she saw Alice getting up and Linda sitting down, oh and Cynthia approaching the table with a glass in her hand, she finally noticed Steph had been missing."

So, she must have been the one in Bert's room, Abby thought.

"Your mom did some more research and discovered Steph owned a restaurant. A few months ago, the restaurant had a couple of cases of food poisoning so the health inspectors shut it down."

"Someone else in need of money," Abby said.

Faith squinted as she read the printout. "She found Steph's full name in one of the social media accounts and the information about the restaurant in a local online newspaper dating back a couple of months. You really have to be careful what goes up online."

"That's all well and good, but we didn't see Steph talking with Robert Howington. We saw Alice. We're going to have to corner her and see if we can squeeze something out of her."

"Because the tactic worked so well with Denise Lowe?" Faith asked.

Abby grabbed a pen and tapped it against her chin. "Denise Lowe mentioned there'd been loans. If Bert organized a loan for Steph, she might have seen her opportunity to have her cake and eat it too. If she got rid of Bert, she wouldn't have to pay back the loan. That would save her a bundle."

"Really? Most people usually shop around for better deals."

"It's strange," Abby said. "From the start, I'd been thinking the person I thought I saw in Bert's room might have been having an affair with him."

Faith settled down on the couch with the laptop. "I'm going to spend some time on those social media pages your mom found. Maybe I can find something she missed. Although, that's highly unlikely."

Yes, Abby agreed. Despite all her efforts to keep her mom in the dark, she'd turned out to be quite helpful and forgiving. Of course, she could be biding her time and waiting for an appropriate moment to tell Abby she should pack her bags and flee for her life before she became a statistic.

"I might have to dash out and get some more photos printed," Faith said.

"What did you find?"

Faith scooped in a breath. "I'm not sure. I've been looking at the group photos from the gardening club.

They're all in different gardens." Faith turned the laptop so Abby could see. "Do you notice anything?"

Abby looked from one person to the other. After a moment, she looked up at the wall and at the first photo she'd taken of the group. "Alice and Linda are always standing next to Bert."

"Yes."

Abby leaned forward. "There are always two other people between Steph and Bert. Almost like a buffer."

Faith clicked her fingers. "That's it." She pointed at one photo and then the other and the other.

"We didn't want to be too obvious about it," Abby said under her breath.

"What are you talking about?" Faith asked.

"I just remembered something Cynthia said when we saw her outside Bert's room. Now that mom has singled Steph out as the one person missing from the group that first night, I bet anything she's the one I saw opening the door."

Had Steph been having an affair with Bert? Worse. Had she used the affair as a way to get close to him and slowly poison him? Abby needed to bite the bullet and call Joshua. He could use his police resources to find out if Steph had borrowed money from Bert. With her restaurant out of action, she would have been in need of money.

"Surprised to hear from me again, detective?" Abby asked.

"Denise Lowe has lodged a formal complaint against you," Joshua said. "For harassment."

"Hello to you too."

"When I spoke with Denise Lowe, her voice hitched," Joshua continued. "Whatever you said really got to her."

"Well then, my job is done. Hang on, I'm feeling a pang of guilt now." Denise Lowe might have come across as a woman of steel, but what if that really had been her way of coping with her loss?

"Think of this as a lesson, Abby Maguire. You have to learn to live with collateral damage or be careful whose feathers you ruffle."

"Duly noted, detective. Now, can you tap into your resources and find out if Steph had taken out a loan?" She explained the rest of her theory and finished by saying, "If she had the most to gain by Bert's death, she would have been smart to stay in the background."

"By the way, you can tell Faith we've checked everyone's phone records. No one made any calls."

"None? That's odd. I know they're all on vacation, but surely they keep in touch with family." Frowning, Abby tried to remember something. "Hang on. I remember coming up for a sweater and walking past one of the rooms. I heard someone talking."

Faith picked up Abby's second new cell phone and waved it.

Biting her bottom lip, Abby nodded in agreement. "You'll have to dig deeper, detective. Someone must have a second phone. Hang on. Does this mean you looked into Robert Howington too?"

"Yes, as much as it hurts me to admit it. There are no records of him getting in touch with any of the tourists. Of course, now I have to dig deeper and make sure there isn't a second phone. I guess my work is cut out. I'll call you back."

Abby gave a slow shake of her head. "That's amazing. Joshua just told me he'd call me back and he's following the lead. When did he become so co-operative?"

"Are you complaining?"

"I'm a lifestyle reporter," Abby said under her breath.

~

"Markus!" Abby sprung to her feet.

"What about him?" Faith asked.

"He's the one who first mentioned Steph missing from the group the day I was attacked. Now I'm thinking Steph might have seen Denise Lowe and her brother leaving and realized she could grab her chance to go back inside Bert's room, but then she found me and… hit me over the head."

Doyle leaped off the couch and scurried toward the door. When Abby heard him whine, she asked, "What's up, Doyle?" he looked at her over his shoulder and then went back to sniffing the door.

"I think there might be someone at the door," Faith whispered.

Abby tiptoed to the door and pressed her ear to it. Making sure Doyle stepped out of the way, she scooped in a breath and wrenched the door open. Propelling herself forward, she caught sight of someone disappearing down the hallway.

Doyle took off and Abby chased after him. When they reached the stairs, Abby came up against a solid chest. "Markus."

"Are you trying to kill yourself?" he barked.

Abby tried to look over his shoulder. "Did you see someone going down the stairs?"

"Yeah. Two women."

~

"Alice and Linda." Abby growled. Markus had taken hold of her and pushed her back saying he would round them up.

"What if they made their escape?" Faith asked.

"They don't have cars. Where would they go?" Abby raked her fingers through her hair. "I should have gone downstairs with him."

The door opened. Markus waved Alice and Linda in. Neither one looked pleased.

"You have no right," Alice said.

"Tell that to the police. They're on their way," Markus said.

Faith held up her phone and mouthed something about calling them now.

"You were outside my apartment eavesdropping," Abby accused. "Why?" They looked at each other but didn't say anything. "Fine. We can wait until the police arrive."

Linda wrung her hands together. "I didn't do anything."

Abby looked at Alice but she refused to meet her gaze. "What about you? Are you going to plead innocent too? If you own up to your role in Bert's death, the police will go easy on you."

They exchanged a look and then Alice groaned. "We had nothing to do with it."

"Then who did?"

Again, they looked at each other. Alice shook her head. The gesture was barely perceptible but Abby wasn't fooled. "You know something."

"We... We weren't sure but we thought Steph might have been having an affair with Bert," Alice said. "Then the police started asking about Foxglove plants. We all grow it in our gardens. A while back, Steph asked me about drying herbs."

"I knew it. You showed her how it's done." That wouldn't be enough proof, Abby thought. "Why were you trying to eavesdrop?"

"We heard stories about you snooping around and thought you might know something." Alice took a deep swallow. "I saw you take a photo of me the other day. I don't want any trouble."

"Well, in that case, you should be more forthcoming with information."

When Alice bit the edge of her lip Abby decided she looked worried enough to now start spilling everything she knew. Thinking Alice needed some further inducement, Abby said, "Faith and I saw you talking with Robert Howington. We have the proof."

The two women exchanged a look again. "A while back, Robert Howington came to one of our barbecues and he started talking about the plants in our gardens and asking questions about poisonous plants."

"And you didn't mention it to anyone?"

"Why would I? I thought he was only making conversation."

~

Markus strode in carrying a tray of coffee and pastries. "There's no sign of Steph."

"She's made a run for it," Abby said. But where would she go?

"It's out of your hands now, Abby. You just have to sit back and let Joshua do his job," her mom said. "He'll track her down."

Yes, but would he also connect her to Robert Howington? "I really don't like coincidences. Why would he ask about poisonous plants? He must have been planning something." Would Joshua find proof? "Joshua will need to get a confession out of Steph."

"She's made herself look suspicious by running away," her mom offered.

True. She'd have to explain herself. Innocent people didn't hide. Abby sprung to her feet. "She's hiding somewhere. Without a car and being out here in the middle of nowhere, she can't hope to get away." Abby grabbed her cell phone and called Joshua.

"Can't talk now, Abby," he said. "We managed to track down a pre-paid phone registered to Steph and another one under Robert's name."

Before she could get a word in, Joshua disconnected the call.

Faith grinned. "See, Eleanor. Abby's never in real danger. She might snoop around but Joshua is the one putting his neck on the line."

"Is that meant to reassure me?" her mom asked.

"Um, yes."

Abby turned to Markus. "Have you checked Steph's room?"

He snorted. "Of course."

"And?"

"There's no sign of her. I even checked under the bed."

Walking around in a tight circle, Abby nibbled on the tip of her thumb.

"Do you think Joshua will be able to track her down using her phone?" Faith asked.

"Most likely," Abby mused. "As long as a phone connects to a carrier's cellular network, the carrier has to keep records of locations."

"Yes, but how accurate are they?"

Abby shrugged. "From what I understand, a person's location can be mapped out on a computer screen to within a few blocks."

Abby's mom cleared her throat. "That's in an urban area, Abby. You're out in the country. So, they'll only be able to track her signal to a few miles."

Abby looked out the window. The sun had already set. If Steph had taken refuge somewhere, she'd have to survive the night.

"What's going through your mind, Abby?" Faith asked.

"If Steph had clandestine meetings with Bert, that would have been the perfect opportunity for her to give him the digitalis. I can picture her sneaking into his room at the end of the day to share a cup of tea. She'd prepare it for him and then take away the evidence with her."

"But she must have slipped up at least once," Faith said. "Leaving a teabag behind."

"What teabag?" her mom asked.

Grinning, Faith said, "Eleanor, Abby has this theory about Steph mixing the digitalis in a teabag."

"That doesn't sound so farfetched. Abby, do you remember me saying someone dropped a serviette over the cell phone a couple of times?" her mom asked.

"Yes. That first day you went out with the tourist group."

"Now that I think about it," her mom continued, "Steph had been closest to the cell phone. She might have been trying to make sure I didn't see her getting up to no good."

Hearing police sirens in the distance, everyone stood up.

"Should we do something?" Faith asked.

Markus was the first one out the door. Faith followed. Grabbing the cell phone and signaling to Doyle, Abby brought up the rear.

"The sirens are getting closer." Faith hurried down the hallway.

"Be careful, Abby," her mom said.

Abby tried to catch up but then stopped and called out to Markus.

"What?"

She signaled to a door. "Is this Steph's room?" she whispered.

Markus nodded.

Abby gestured for him to open the door.

"Why?" Markus mouthed as he unlocked the door.

Abby peered inside. She nudged the door open so the light from the hallway could spill in. The room was empty. Tiptoeing toward the window, she felt Markus following a step behind. In the time she'd been living at the pub, she hadn't once looked up at her window from the street. She hadn't even noticed the fire escape ladders.

Edging closer to the window, she looked down and sprung back.

"What?" Markus whispered.

Abby grabbed him by the arm and drew him out of the room and down the stairs.

"Would you mind telling me what that was about?"

"I found Steph."

~

They all piled out of the pub and went to stand at the corner. The police car sirens had stopped but they could see the lights still whirling around a block away.

"I'm guessing they caught up with Robert Howington," Abby said. Looking over her shoulder, she saw Markus standing by the gates leading to the alleyway, a cell phone to his ear, probably Mitch's, Abby thought knowing Markus didn't own a cell phone. Abby had agreed to let him do the honors and call the police.

While they didn't have any concrete proof, Abby could only think of one reason for Steph to hide. Guilt.

"Is that Joshua walking toward us?" Faith asked.

"I think so. I guess he didn't want to alert Steph." Abby looked over her shoulder just as Markus growled.

"She's going back up the ladder," he called out.

"You're kidding."

"Abby, what's going on?" her mom asked. "Why are we bouncing?"

"Steph is trying to make another getaway." Abby trotted toward the residents' entrance calling out to Faith to ring Mitch who'd stayed in the pub.

Someone must have alerted Joshua too because he called out. "Abby. Stand back."

"What?" Abby made the mistake of looking toward him just as she reached the residents' entrance.

Steph burst out and crashed against her.

"Ugh! You," Steph growled. She pushed Abby and took off running in the opposite direction.

Abby fell back on her butt. "Ouch and... Really? She thinks she's going to outrun a police officer?" In the next instant, Joshua sped by, followed by Faith and Markus.

"I'm fine. Thank you for asking."

Epilogue

"I'm exhausted," her mom exclaimed later that night. "I'll have so many stories to tell. I can't wait for you to send me the photos so I can have a show and tell. Everyone wants to hear about my trip. I'll need another vacation after this. A real one."

"I'm counting on it," Abby said. "You know you'll be safe coming here for a visit. What are the chances of someone else being killed?"

"Abby, that's tempting fate," her mom warned. A moment later, her mom hummed. "I'd hate to say this, but a part of me is still in denial and waiting for you to tell me all is well and Bert had gone along with a hoax."

"Sorry to disappoint you, Mom. Unfortunately, it was all too real but you must admit, it had to be coincidental."

"I thought you said you don't like coincidences."

True. "Oh, look. Here comes Joshua."

Everyone at the bar fell silent. Joshua made a beeline for Abby's table and drew out a chair.

"Well, that's that," he said.

They all leaned in.

"Now, can you fill in all the gaps?" Abby asked.

He grinned. "What's there to say?"

"He's going to make us beg," Markus growled.

"Or guess," Abby said.

Joshua grinned. "You want to try that?"

"The cell phone gave you an idea of Robert Howington's whereabouts," Faith piped in. "I should clarify, this is the second cell phone Abby insisted he had to have. Oh, and I should add further clarification by saying this is the man Abby suspected of colluding with someone because she saw him talking with one of the tourists. We have to give her credit. After all, she went out on a limb."

"Fine." Joshua put his hand up. "I'll come clean. Abby's suspicions sometimes sound farfetched but, in this case, they turned out to be spot on. We intercepted Robert Howington and followed at a discreet distance. Then, he must have noticed we were following, so we had to give chase. Now, I want to know how you discovered Steph had been clinging to the fire escape ladder, hoping to go unnoticed until she could meet up with Robert Howington and make her getaway."

"Abby used deductive thinking," her mom said.

"The small town is surrounded by miles of countryside. Where else could she have gone?" Faith reasoned and turned to Abby for confirmation.

Abby could only nod. In reality, she had thought of the fire escape ladder because that would have been the last place she would choose to hide in. "So, who was the mastermind?"

Joshua brushed his hand across his face. "Steph gave a statement saying Robert had approached her with the plan."

"That's the part I don't quite understand," Abby mused. "If someone approaches me with a suggestion we pull our resources and get rid of someone, I'd tell them to take a hike."

"I guess Robert tapped into her need," Joshua said. "He knew she'd run into financial difficulties. Her restaurant had been shut down so she didn't have any means of earning a living. At her age, it would be near impossible to recoup her loses. He offered her a couple of million dollars. That would be enough to tempt anyone."

"Yes, but who had the idea of mixing the digitalis with the tea?" Abby asked. Mostly, she wanted to know who'd hit her on the head, but she couldn't ask because her mom was hanging on every word and the incident remained the one fact she had managed to keep secret. She could only assume it had been Steph.

"Robert masterminded the plan. He needed the money and he couldn't wait until his dad died of natural causes. Apparently, his dad had been rethinking the will and had considered reducing the amount of money he left his son. That gave Robert incentive to put his plan into motion. He knew his dad had the women wrapped around his little finger. They were like bees to honey and all vying for his attention. He convinced Steph he would never offer her more than a fling before moving on to the next one. Steph is only saying she saw an opportunity and grabbed it. Robert Howington knew his dad's medication was constantly being monitored and rightly assumed upsetting the balance would have an adverse effect."

Abby's mom sighed. "Bert seemed so nice. I find it hard to believe he had been flitting from one woman to another."

Abby wished she could put her arms around her mom. In reality, she knew there had to be some truth to Bert's behavior. Cynthia had admitted he had only recently started singling her out for private *tête-à-têtes*. She would have been his next conquest...

"I can't help feeling sorry for Steph," Abby's mom said.

"She'd already had a few bad relationships," Joshua told her. "So, she'd become embittered. When Robert told Steph his father would never offer her a serious commitment, she settled for the next best thing."

"Murder?" Abby exclaimed. "That's rather extreme."

Her mom shook her head. "That's an act of desperation. It's sad to think someone could reach that point."

Abby snatched Markus' order book and scrawled on it, asking Joshua if Steph had owned up to hitting her on the head. When he read it, he gave her a small nod. Finally, she thought. The mystery of her attacker solved.

"How did they ever think they would get away with murder?"

"Robert Howington assumed his dad's death wouldn't draw attention because he'd had a pre-existing condition. And, he was right, up to a point. Unfortunately for him, we might live in a small town but we have competent staff working at the hospital. If only we'd been able to get our hands on that one teabag." Joshua smiled. "Steph had planned on delivering the fatal dosage. She prepared the tea for Bert, but then she forgot to retrieve the teabag until the next day."

Aha. That made sense. Abby nodded and mouthed, "Thank you."

"Such a tragedy," her mom said. "No one deserves to have their life cut short."

"Have you spoken with Denise Lowe?" Abby asked.

Joshua nodded. "I found that difficult. The woman didn't bat an eyelid. On the bright side, she said she'd been through enough so she won't be contesting her dad's will or his promise to give Eleanor the drawing. I think that might be her way of expressing her gratitude to you, Abby." Joshua clasped his hands and turned his attention to the cell phone. "So, Eleanor. When can we hope to meet you in person?"

To Abby's surprise, her mom gave an uncharacteristic snort. "Well, my virtual tour doesn't end for a few more days. Anything could happen between now and then. Although, I have to say, surely the town has already had its fair share of mishaps. What are the chances of someone else being murdered?"

~

Printed in Great Britain
by Amazon